E-mail mix-up!

MICHELLE

Michelle has a plan to get Stephanie to notice her shy next door neighbor, Ted Bailey the Third. Ted totally likes Stephanie—and Michelle is convinced that he would be Stephanie's perfect date for the annual class picnic.

So Michelle convinces Ted to send Stephanie an anonymous e-mail from TB03—his e-mail address—telling her how much he likes her. Michelle figures that something as romantic as that is sure to get Ted and Stephanie together!

STEPHANIE

Stephanie is totally thrilled when she receives a romantic e-mail from TB03—because that could only be the e-mail address of one person—Todd Barnes! He's tall, totally cute, *and* he's number 03—the all-star captain of the John Muir Middle School basketball team!

Stephanie starts hanging out with Todd—and begins to see a different side of him. He doesn't seem very romantic—or even very interested in her. He's a way different person than he is in his e-mail!

Which makes Stephanie wonder, which is the real Todd Barnes?

FULL HOUSE™: SISTERS books

Two on the Town
One Boss Too Many
And the Winner Is . . .
How to Hide a Horse
Problems in Paradise
Will You Be My Valentine?
Let's Put On a Show!
Baby-sitters and Company
Substitute Sister
Ask Miss Know-It-All
Matchmakers
No Rules Weekend
   (Coming in February 2001)

Available from MINSTREL Books

FULL HOUSE™
Sisters

Matchmakers

DIANA G. GALLAGHER

A Parachute Press Book

A
MINSTREL®
BOOK

Published by POCKET BOOKS
New York   London   Toronto   Sydney   Singapore

This book is a work of fiction. Names, characters, places and incidents are products of the author's imagination or are used fictitiously. Any resemblance to actual events or locales or persons living or dead is entirely coincidental.

A MINSTREL PAPERBACK *Original*

A Minstrel Book published by
POCKET BOOKS, a division of Simon & Schuster, Inc.
1230 Avenue of the Americas, New York, NY 10020

A PARACHUTE PRESS BOOK

Copyright © and ™ 2000 by Warner Bros.

FULL HOUSE, characters, names and all related indicia are trademarks of Warner Bros. © 2000.

ISBN: 0-671-04091-X

First Minstrel Books printing December 2000

10 9 8 7 6 5 4 3 2 1

A MINSTREL BOOK and colophon are registered trademarks of Simon & Schuster, Inc.

Printed in the U.S.A.

STEPHANIE

Chapter
1

Yes! We're free!" Stephanie cheered. She pushed through the doors of John Muir Middle School and sucked in a deep breath of spring air. Her two best friends, Allie Taylor and Darcy Powell, followed close behind her.

It was two-thirty on Wednesday afternoon, and that meant there were only two more days of school before the weekend.

"Didn't that seem like the longest school day in history?" Stephanie asked her friends.

"Absolutely," Darcy agreed, pushing a dark curl off her forehead. "I couldn't wait for the bell to ring—except when we were in that assembly about the annual class picnic."

"I know what you mean. The picnic is going to be totally fun this year," Stephanie said. "I was assigned to chip and dip detail. What did you volunteer to bring, Allie?"

"You mean besides my imaginary date?" Allie's green eyes sparkled at her own joke. "Potato salad."

Stephanie grinned. "Don't give up hope yet. The picnic isn't until a week from Saturday. There's still plenty of time for the two of us to get dates."

Stephanie and her friends had gone to the annual class picnic without dates for the past two years. *But this year,* Stephanie thought, *it would be nice to have a special someone to share the potato-sack races and egg-tossing tournaments with—not to mention the romantic picnic lunch.* Especially since Darcy would be sharing the day with her brand-new boyfriend, Doug.

"Hey you guys, you don't need dates," Darcy said. "Doug won't mind hanging out with all of us."

Allie shrugged. She adjusted the sparkly headband in her light brown hair. "No offense, Darce, but two's company and four is just too many."

"Right." Stephanie nodded. "I mean, Doug's a really cool guy, but even he won't appreciate your friends hanging around all day."

"Hey!" Darcy interrupted. She pointed to the basketball courts in the school yard. "Check it out!"

Stephanie followed Darcy's gaze. The John Muir Middle School basketball team was having a pickup game—playing just for fun. Todd Barnes, team captain and star forward, seemed to be tearing up the court—as usual.

"Come on! Let's watch for a while," Stephanie suggested.

The girls made their way through the tightly packed crowd to stand on the sidelines.

Stephanie found her eyes glued to Todd as he dribbled effortlessly down the court. Soon he was blocked by opponents on all sides. "He's got nowhere to go," Stephanie said, shaking her head. "He'll never get out of this one."

The words had barely left Stephanie's mouth when Todd faked left. He did a 360 to the right and broke out into the open. He tossed the ball to a teammate and sprinted down court.

The teammate tossed the ball back. Todd caught it and took a shot from the foul line.

The ball arched through the air and swooshed into the basket. Score!

The spectators whistled, cheered, and applauded. Todd punched the air with his fist and kept playing.

"Whoa. Todd is so cool," Darcy said. "He looks practically professional out there."

"And totally cute," Allie added with a wistful gaze. "I sure wouldn't mind having a date with *him*."

Neither would I, Stephanie thought as Todd dribbled around two guards and made a fantastic jump shot.

Tall and tan with short blond hair and brown eyes, Todd was incredibly good-looking. But,

Stephanie realized, Todd had never talked to her—or her friends. He probably didn't even know who they were.

"Heads up!" one of the players shouted. The basketball sailed out-of-bounds—right at Stephanie. She put up her hands to shield herself and caught the ball. Surprised, Stephanie looked up, wondering who she should toss it to.

Todd Barnes was standing directly in front of her.

Stephanie gazed into his brown eyes for a second, then handed the ball over.

"Thanks, Stephanie." Todd gave her a crooked grin. "Nice catch."

As Todd made his way back into the game, Stephanie felt Allie grip her arm. "Oh my gosh!" her friend whispered. "How does Todd Barnes know your name?"

"I—I have no idea," Stephanie stuttered.

"I bet he likes you," Darcy concluded.

Stephanie shook her head. "Don't be silly. He just heard my name somewhere at school, that's all. Or maybe he read one of my articles in the *Scribe*."

Stephanie wrote for John Muir Middle School's newspaper. Her picture appeared next to her name at the beginning of each of her articles. *That has to be it*, Stephanie reasoned.

But deep inside she felt a thrill go through her. Wouldn't it be great if Todd knew her name because he'd noticed her—and liked her?

For just a second Stephanie pictured herself dating the cutest, most popular, most athletic guy at school. She sighed wistfully. It was certainly a nice dream.

"Hey, Stephanie!" a boy's voice called.

Stephanie snapped out of her thoughts. Ted Bailey the Third (that was how he had introduced himself to her) was standing on the sidelines at the opposite end of the court. He waved enthusiastically at her.

She grinned and waved back. "Hi, Ted!"

The boy began to move toward her—directly across the court, into the middle of the game!

"No, wait!" Stephanie began, but it was too late.

"Ooof!" Ted cried as one of the basketball players barreled into him. He hit the ground hard.

Several of the players crouched down to see if he was okay. Soon they had Ted up and walking around the court, making sure he wasn't in any pain. "I'm okay," Ted said, shrugging them off. "Really, I'm fine."

"Uh-oh, Stephanie," Paula Warner said. The ultrapopular, auburn-haired captain of the cheerleading squad was standing right next to Darcy. Like Todd, she had hardly ever spoken to Stephanie and her friends.

Paula leaned closer. "If you hurry, you can get away before Ted actually makes it over here to talk to you," she whispered.

Stephanie bristled. "For your information," she told Paula, "Ted is a great guy."

"You mean . . . you actually *know* him?" Paula asked, sounding shocked.

"Yeah. Ted moved in next door to me last month," Stephanie reported. "He's very nice and incredibly smart. If you ever talked to him, maybe you'd know that."

Stephanie knew that Ted was having a hard time fitting in at John Muir Middle School. He was a little uncomfortable when he spoke—and he was pretty clumsy on his feet.

Not exactly a recipe for instant popularity, she realized. But Stephanie thought Ted's shy manner was adorable—in a little lost puppy sort of way.

"Whatever." Paula shrugged. "But, hey, if you do get to talk to your new friend, let him know that he needs a haircut." She wiggled her fingers in farewell and walked away.

Stephanie winced. She had to admit that Ted wasn't exactly at the head of the class style-wise, either. His too-long brown hair was always falling into his eyes, which were covered by thick, dark-framed glasses. He was a little thin and usually wore flannel shirts and jeans.

But appearance doesn't mean everything, Stephanie told herself. *Right?*

"Paula can be so rude," Darcy observed after the girl had left.

8

"Yeah. Ted *is* nice," Allie agreed. "Even if he is a little—uh—different."

Aside from his less-than-cool appearance, Ted tended to have unusual interests, Stephanie recalled. He liked watching sci-fi shows on late-night television. And he loved fixing computers, taking them apart and changing around the components inside.

None of which would be so bad, Stephanie thought, *if he didn't talk about sci-fi and computers all the time*. It made him seem a little on the nerdy side.

"Oh, gosh!" Darcy glanced at her watch. "I've got to go. My mom's waiting to take me shopping for new shoes."

"Wait for me," Allie said. She hitched her book bag securely on to her back. "Want to come with us, Stephanie?"

"Not this time, guys. I've got to pick Michelle up at school," Stephanie explained. "I'll take a rain check, though. And I'll call you both later, okay?"

Sometimes Michelle, Stephanie's younger sister, walked home from Fraser Elementary with her friends. Other times someone in the extended Tanner family picked her up at the end of the day. There were a *lot* of people in the family to share the job.

When Stephanie's mom died, Stephanie's dad, Danny, asked his best friend, Joey Gladstone, and his brother-in-law, Jesse, to move into his house. Uncle Jesse and Joey helped Danny take care of his three daughters, D.J., Stephanie, and Michelle.

Then Uncle Jesse married Aunt Becky. The two of them moved into an apartment in the attic of Stephanie's house. A few years later Aunt Becky and Uncle Jesse had twin boys, Nicky and Alex. That made nine people in one very full house!

Stephanie waved good-bye to Allie and Darcy, then noticed Ted moving toward her again. "Hi, Stephanie!" he said, stopping beside her.

"Hi!" Stephanie greeted him. "Are you okay? You really got tackled out there."

Ted nodded. "I'm fine," he said, his mouth pressed into a tight smile. "Are you, uh, going home now?"

"Yeah, but I have to pick Michelle up first," Stephanie reported. "Do you want to walk together? I'd love the company—if you don't mind a short detour to Fraser Elementary."

"No. I mean, yeah. I mean—okay!" Ted finally spit out the words.

Stephanie smiled. It was great having someone to talk to on the walk home. And besides being a nice guy, Ted was a great listener. Stephanie didn't care what people like Paula said. She was glad to be Ted's friend.

She glanced back one more time at Todd Barnes. *He really is cute,* she thought with a sigh.

Stephanie and Ted turned from the game and made their way down the sidewalk. "So—have you started your paper for science yet?" Stephanie asked. Both she and Ted were in Mrs. Gruen's advanced science class during third period.

"Actually, I'm almost done with it," Ted told her.

"Done?" Stephanie's eyes widened. "But

our papers aren't due until a week from tomorrow!"

"I mean, I'm done with the—uh—research." Ted sounded apologetic, as if he was embarrassed about being ahead of schedule.

"Wow! That's great," Stephanie said. "I took a reference book out of the library, but it hasn't helped me a bit. I'm totally stumped for a topic."

Mrs. Gruen had asked everyone to pick a topic having to do with outer space and write a five-page report on it. But the subject was so broad, Stephanie had no idea where to start.

Ted's eyes lit up. "Two hints: use the Internet for research, and write about the *future* of space technology."

"The future, huh?" Stephanie pretended to scold Ted, wagging her finger at him in an exaggerated way. "Isn't that more like science fiction?"

Ted smiled sheepishly. It was a nice, bright, warm smile.

"Tell the truth," Stephanie teased. "Are you

doing your report on that space show you like—*Star Voyage?*"

Ted laughed and shook his head. "No. My paper is about some totally cool projects NASA is actually working on right now. Like space stations and a mining project on the moon."

Wow! Ted is so enthusiastic about space science he doesn't sound at all awkward or self-conscious when he speaks about it, Stephanie thought. If only he could be this confident and easygoing all the time!

As they reached the doors of Michelle's school, an idea struck her. "Um—Ted? I don't suppose you could come over and help me with my research, could you?" she asked.

"Me?" Ted squeaked. He cleared his throat. "I mean—me? Sure! I know some great space science web sites. When do you want to work on the project?"

"How about tomorrow after school?"

"Absolutely," Ted answered.

Excellent! It would be great hanging out with Ted and having his help on her project. Besides, maybe during their study sessions she could help loosen him up. Then he wouldn't have such a hard time making friends at school.

Stephanie smiled to herself. Before the semester was over, she vowed, Ted was going to go from Mr. Invisible to Mr. Popularity. And she, Stephanie Tanner, was going to make sure it happened!

MICHELLE

Chapter
2

See you later, Cassie. Later, Mandy."
Michelle waved good-bye to her two best
friends and headed out the door of the school.
Her older sister Stephanie was waiting to pick
her up at the bottom of the steps.

Usually Michelle walked home with her
friends or an adult member of her family. It was
a total treat to have Stephanie pick her up.

Walking home with Stephanie made
Michelle feel special. It made her feel as if she
and her sister were hanging out together, just
the two of them.

"Hi, Stephanie!" Michelle called. She ran toward her sister. Then she noticed a boy standing beside Stephanie. It was her new next-door neighbor, Ted. Michelle's smile grew even bigger.

"Hey, Ted! Are you walking home with us?" Michelle asked.

"Well, I guess I could *skip* home with you instead," Ted joked. "But we might look kind of silly."

Michelle laughed. Ted was the absolute best. He always seemed interested in talking to her. And he never treated her like a little kid.

Michelle wedged herself happily between Stephanie and Ted. The three of them headed for home.

"So, Ted, are you planning to go to the picnic next weekend?" Stephanie asked.

"Picnic?" Ted blinked. "Oh, you mean the class picnic. Uh—maybe. Are you?"

"Of course. It's only the coolest event of the year!" Stephanie exclaimed. "Are you planning on asking anyone to go with you?"

Ted stuck his hands in his jeans pockets. "I-I haven't decided yet."

Awesome. Date-talk, Michelle thought.

Ever since Ted moved in, Michelle hoped that one day soon he and Stephanie would start going out. The two of them obviously had a good time together—and Ted was the absolute sweetest. Maybe Michelle's wish was finally coming true.

"Who are *you* going to the picnic with, Stephanie?" she asked.

Michelle's older sister frowned. "Right now, I'm going with Allie and Darcy. And Doug."

"Doug? Who's that?" Michelle wanted to know.

"He's Darcy's new boyfriend," Stephanie answered. "He's this really cute football player. The two of them have been talking on the phone nonstop lately." She sighed. "Now Allie and I are looking for dates, too."

Michelle's mind whirred. Stephanie was going to the picnic—and she didn't have a date. Ted was going to the picnic and . . . hmmm.

"Hey, Ted, if you were going to ask someone to the picnic, who would it be?" Michelle asked, tilting her head.

17

Ted glanced over at Stephanie. His face was slightly pink. "I'm not sure," he replied.

"Oh." Michelle said. *Unless I'm completely crazy, Ted wants to ask Stephanie,* she thought. *And he'd be the perfect guy for Stephanie to take to the school picnic.*

"Well, I have to go," Ted said as they came to their houses. "It was nice walking with you guys!" He sprinted toward his front door.

"Bye!" Michelle waved. She glanced up at her sister. *Hmmm.* Ted was definitely interested in taking Stephanie to the picnic. But was Stephanie interested in going with him? Maybe she should find out for sure.

"So . . . why don't you have a date for the picnic yet?" Michelle asked her sister.

"No one has asked me," Stephanie replied.

Michelle grinned mischievously.

I can make sure that someone asks Stephanie to the picnic. Someone like Ted Bailey. Then Stephanie and Ted would both be happy. What could be better than that?

* * *

"Hi, Ted! What's up?" Michelle said as she let her neighbor into the Tanner house Thursday afternoon.

"Hi, Michelle. Is Stephanie home?" Ted asked, stepping into the living room. He ran his fingers nervously through his shaggy brown hair. "I'm here to help her with her science report."

"Bo-ring!" Michelle said in a singsong voice. "Want to play my new computer game with me instead?" She held up her CD-ROM case. "It's really cool."

" 'Marla's Magical Mystery,' " Ted read the title of the game. "Hey! My younger cousin, Ruth, has this game. It's awesome."

"I know!" Michelle said. "I've played it at my friend Cassie's. It took me weeks of extra chores to save up enough to buy it. My dad finally brought it home for me last night." She paused, wagging the CD-ROM case in front of Ted's nose. "Come on. You *know* you want to play it with me."

Stephanie bounded down the stairs. "No way, Michelle. Ted's all mine—and so is the computer in our room."

Ted glanced up at Stephanie. Michelle was sure she could see a sparkle in his eyes as he gazed at her sister.

He turned and placed a hand on Michelle's shoulder. "Thanks, Michelle, but these term papers Stephanie and I are working on are really important," he explained. "They count for twenty-five percent of our grade this marking period."

"Sorry," Stephanie told her. "You'll have to wait till later to play 'Marla's Magical Mystery.' "

"Actually, I don't have to wait at all," Michelle realized. "We can just use the computer in the study."

"Oh, no." Stephanie shook her head. "That's Dad's computer, and you know you're not allowed to touch it. He's got important work files stored in it. He'd be in big trouble if something accidentally happened to them."

"*I* don't have permission to use Dad's computer," Michelle pointed out, "but you do."

Stephanie hesitated. "Well . . . that's true."

"Don't worry, Stephanie," Ted said. "I'll just write down all the web site addresses for you so you'll be able to find them on your computer later. Then Michelle gets to play her game, and we get to do research. Everybody will be happy!"

"Thanks, Ted." Michelle beamed. She stared hard at Stephanie. "You know, you're *so nice* to help my sister out like this."

Ted shrugged and shoved his hands into his pockets. "No problem." He sneaked another look at Stephanie.

"Okay, then. The computer in the study it is," Stephanie said. "I'll be right back. I just have to run upstairs to get my notebook." Ted's gaze followed her as she jogged upstairs.

"So do you have a date for the class picnic yet?" Michelle asked. *Even though it's completely obvious who you want to go with,* she thought.

Ted's head snapped back around to stare at her. His face turned pink. "Uh, well—no, I guess I don't."

"That's very interesting," Michelle said. "*Stephanie* still doesn't have a date yet, either."

Ted's eyes widened. "Really?"

"Not yet," Michelle whispered. She nudged Ted with her elbow. "Get the picture?"

"Hey, Ted, we'd better get started," Stephanie called. She jogged down the stairs and led the way to the study.

Ted stared at Michelle a second longer, then followed Stephanie into the study.

Michelle raced up to her room. *What a perfect afternoon*, she thought. She had the computer all to herself and hours of free time to play her new game.

And the best part is, Ted got my hint, Michelle thought. She was positive he would ask Stephanie to the class picnic before he went home tonight.

Then Stephanie would have the best date ever. And it would all be thanks to Michelle!

MICHELLE

Chapter 3

That evening, Michelle waited for Stephanie to burst into their room with the news that Ted had asked her to the picnic. After Ted went home, though, Stephanie didn't seem any happier than she had earlier that afternoon—and she didn't mention the picnic at all.

Michelle decided to take matters into her own hands. "So, Stephanie," she prompted as the whole family sat down to dinner, "did Ted help you out with your report this afternoon?"

23

"Totally," Stephanie told her, passing the potatoes. "We got a lot of work done."

"Oh," Michelle said, disappointed. "Just work?"

"You know, that Ted is a great guy," Danny chimed in from his place at the head of the table. "I'm glad you two are getting along so well, Stephanie. He reminds me a lot of me when I was his age."

"Yeah," Joey agreed. "Except I bet Ted's haircut is better than yours ever was."

Joey laughed loudly at his own joke. Uncle Jesse joined in.

"Yeah," he said, feeding Alex a forkful of macaroni. "I saw those old pictures, Danny. Your crew cut was buzzed so short, you looked bald!"

"Hey, leave Danny alone," Aunt Becky scolded him. She poured Nicky a cup of juice. "I'll bet that look was very cool at the time."

"Sure," Joey answered. "If you were in the army." Everyone at the table burst out laughing again.

Better get this conversation back on track,

Michelle thought. "So you didn't talk to Ted about anything besides your report?" she pressed Stephanie.

"Well, we did clown around a little," Stephanie admitted. "Ted's a totally funny guy. Oh, and Ted did give me a lecture about how much faster his computer is than Dad's. He said it had something to do with the processor."

"That's true, Dad," D.J., Michelle's oldest sister, agreed. She took a sip of her water. "Compared to the computers we have at college, yours is sluggish."

"I know." Danny nodded. "I've been meaning to upgrade my processor. I've just been too busy to get to it." He paused, thinking. "You know, Ted's really good with computers. Maybe I'll ask him to help me do it."

Disappointed, Michelle tuned out the rest of the conversation. So Ted hadn't asked Stephanie to the picnic at all. Instead, he wimped out!

Michelle frowned. Maybe getting Ted together with her sister was going to be harder than she thought. It seemed as if Ted needed a stronger push to get things started.

That's okay, Michelle figured. *There's still time until the picnic. And tomorrow I'm definitely going to make sure Ted gets the picture about Stephanie.*

After dinner Michelle helped clear the table. Then she ran back upstairs, anxious to return to her game. She had almost gotten through level one of 'Marla's Magical Mystery' that afternoon. She wanted to reach level two before she went to bed.

When Michelle walked into her room, Stephanie was already sitting at the computer. "How long are you going to be using that?" Michelle asked.

"Not much longer," Stephanie sat back with a frustrated sigh. "I wanted to find some of the sites Ted gave me, but I think there's something wrong with our Internet connection."

"I didn't touch *anything* except my game," Michelle said. "Honest."

"I wasn't going to blame you, Michelle."

Stephanie smiled. "Anyway, now that we've got Ted-the-expert living next door, it could be that our family's computer problems are over."

Michelle flopped down on her bed. *Maybe I should point out some of Ted's other excellent qualities to Stephanie,* she thought. That might move the whole date thing along a little faster.

"Ted can fix anything," Michelle said. "I think he's a genius."

"Mmm-hmmm." Stephanie didn't glance up at all.

"Also, he's always totally nice to me," she added.

"Yup." Stephanie jotted something down in her notebook.

Michelle switched to a different approach. "So—it's too bad you don't have a date for the class picnic."

Stephanie shrugged. "The picnic isn't for more than a week. There's still time. And if I don't have a date, it's no big deal."

Michelle frowned. Wasn't anyone able to take a hint around here?

The doorbell rang downstairs. Stephanie

leaped up from her seat. "Are we having company?" Michelle asked.

"It's Darcy and Allie," Stephanie answered. "We're going to watch a movie tonight, so the computer's all yours." She closed her book and switched off the computer's Internet service. "Have fun!" she called on her way out the door.

"I will," Michelle answered. She put Ted and Stephanie out of her mind for the moment and rushed over to the computer. Comet, the family's golden retriever, entered the room. He padded over and settled on the floor beside Michelle's chair.

Michelle popped her game disk into the CD-ROM drive. 'Marla's Magical Mystery' blinked onto the screen. Michelle hit the RESUME button to continue the game she had been playing.

Soon she had found the treasure and defeated all of the monsters on level two. But to get to level three, Michelle had to get rid of a tremendous, scary monster-dog that was guarding a door. So far, she couldn't figure out how to do it.

She stopped Marla two squares from the monster-dog. She squinted at the screen, thinking hard. How could she get around it?

Comet made a whining sound at her feet. "What is it, Comet?" Michelle asked. "Do you know how to get rid of the monster?" Comet's tail thumped against the floor. He looked at Michelle with big, brown eyes.

Michelle scratched him behind the ears. "Maybe a snack will inspire us," she said.

She paused the game, stood up, and stretched. Joey had made cupcakes with strawberry icing that afternoon. And right now her stomach was crying out for one.

Michelle jogged down the stairs. Comet followed, hoping for a doggie treat.

Stephanie, Darcy, and Allie sat on the sofa in the living room, talking. Michelle waved to them and turned toward the kitchen.

"Come on, Stephanie," Allie said. "Get real. You can't tell us you wouldn't just *love* to go to the class picnic with Todd Barnes."

Michelle stopped short. Uh-oh. Who was Todd Barnes?

Stephanie laughed. "I guess that might be interesting."

"Interesting?" Darcy glanced at Allie, then back at Stephanie. "Let's see. Todd's the captain of the basketball team, totally cute, and the most popular boy in school. *Fantastic* is the word you're looking for—not *interesting*."

"Okay, so it would be fantastic," Stephanie agreed.

Oh, no. Michelle's spirits sank as she hurried into the kitchen. Stephanie liked someone named Todd Barnes! But how was that possible when Ted was obviously the perfect match for her?

Ted was nice and funny and smart and *everything* Stephanie liked in a boy. True, he wasn't on the basketball team. And he hadn't been at school long enough to be very popular yet, either.

Michelle had hinted that Ted should ask Stephanie out. Major mistake!

What if Ted does ask Stephanie to the picnic, and she says no? Michelle worried.

Her mind raced as she grabbed a cupcake and ran back upstairs. Michelle didn't know how she was going to do it, but she had to make sure Ted and Stephanie ended up going to that picnic together.

And I can't waste any time, she realized. *Because if Ted doesn't ask Stephanie to go to the picnic soon, Todd might ask her first!*

Chapter
4

Friday in the cafeteria, Stephanie ate lunch at her usual table with Darcy and Allie. Actually, she wasn't eating, she realized. She was just stirring her yogurt around with her spoon.

While her two friends talked about their morning classes, Stephanie stared over their shoulders at Todd Barnes and his friends from the basketball team. They sat at a table directly across from Stephanie's.

He's so totally cute, Stephanie thought. *I wonder what it would be like to go on a date with him.*

"Hello . . . Stephanie!" Darcy waved her

hand in front of Stephanie's face. "Didn't you hear a word I said?"

Stephanie snapped out of her thoughts. She felt her face flush red.

"What have you been staring at?" Allie wondered. She glanced over her shoulder. She caught sight of Todd and raised her eyebrows at her friend. "Stephanie . . . I think you're developing a major crush here."

"Yeah." Stephanie sighed. "You're right. Me and about a hundred other girls have a crush on Todd Barnes."

"Well, I think you should go over to him and say something," Darcy stated. "I mean, why not?"

"Yeah, *why not?*" Stephanie asked. She rose from her seat.

"Wh-What are you doing?" Allie stuttered.

"Exactly what Darcy suggested," Stephanie stated. She took a deep breath and let it out with a whoosh. "Wish me luck."

"You go, girl!" Darcy cheered Stephanie on.

"Just remember, think 'cool,' " Allie coached.

Cool. Stephanie thought. *Okay—I'll just get a*

soda from the vending machine. On my way by I'll say, "Hi, Todd" or, "What's up, Todd?" Or maybe I'll just nod in his direction.

She took a few steps toward Todd's table. He glanced up and their eyes met.

This is it! she thought.

"Hey, Stephanie!" a voice called from behind her.

Stephanie turned to see Ted Bailey walking toward her with his lunch tray.

"I just wanted to tell you I—whoa!" Ted's sentence was cut off as he tripped over his untied shoelace. His tray tipped toward Stephanie.

She watched as the scene seemed to unfold in slow motion. Ted's open chocolate milk container flew at her.

Splash! It spilled all over her white cotton blouse.

"Yuck!" Stephanie cried. Her shirt, her face—*everything* dripped with the thick, brown liquid.

"Oh, Stephanie, I'm so sorry!" Ted cried. He grabbed some napkins from a nearby table and offered them to her.

Stephanie glanced toward Todd's table. Todd and his friends were laughing their heads off. *I can't believe it*, Stephanie thought. *My cool and casual moment is completely ruined.*

"I hope you're not mad, Stephanie," Ted continued. "I mean, I am really sorry."

"Not as sorry as I am," Stephanie responded. "Definitely not as sorry as I am."

Friday afternoon at home, Stephanie peered outside her window. She saw Ted down below, holding a green garden hose. He was watering the grass outside his house.

Ah-ha! There he is, she thought. She sped down the stairs and out the front door.

"Ted! We need to talk," Stephanie called. She walked up to him and grabbed him by the sleeve. She dragged him toward the Tanner house.

"Hey!" Ted yelped. "Listen, if you're still mad at me, I can buy you a new shirt or something."

"What?" Stephanie asked. She shook her head. "Oh, no. I'm sorry. I'm not angry at you, Ted, really."

"Whew. That's a relief." Ted wiped his brow dramatically.

Stephanie couldn't help but smile. "I'm not mad . . . but you do owe me for making me look like a fool in front of the entire school, right?"

Ted nodded and cleared his throat. "I— uh—I guess so."

"Great!" Stephanie smiled. "You're the only computer expert I know, Ted, and my Internet connection is in big trouble. Can you help me?"

"Sure," Ted said.

"Fantastic!" Stephanie cheered. She led him into the house and upstairs to her room.

Inside she saw that Michelle had taken her place at the computer desk.

"Hey, Michelle," Ted called as he walked over to the desk.

Michelle smiled when Ted peered over her shoulder at the computer screen. "Hey, Ted. This is my new game. Totally cool, huh?"

Ted nodded. "Great graphics. You're almost done with level two? I'm impressed."

"Me, too." Michelle giggled. She glanced

past Ted at Stephanie. "Do you guys need the computer?"

"Yup," Stephanie said. "Ted's going to fix the Internet problem."

"No problem." Michelle saved her place in the game, then exited the program.

Whoa. What was going on here? Stephanie had expected Michelle to argue at least a *little* about giving up the computer. Instead she put her game CD in its case and stood up.

"Homework first. That's the rule," Michelle said. "I'll just go watch TV or something." She left the room, taking her CD case with her. "You guys have fun," she called over her shoulder.

Stephanie stared after her sister. *That was too easy*, she thought. *And what was with the "have fun" comment?*

She shrugged. If there was one thing living with a younger sister had taught her, it was not to take every nutty thing Michelle said too seriously.

"So what's the message you're getting on your screen?" Ted asked as he slid into the desk chair.

Stephanie pulled over a folding chair and sat down beside him. She logged on to her on-line account, then sat back to give Ted room to work. "Connection time something."

"Connection timed out." Ted nodded. "Your browser probably needs to be updated. I can adjust the speed settings, too."

"You're the expert." Stephanie watched as Ted opened a window she had never seen before. *Ted really is amazing with this stuff*, she thought.

After Ted had typed some commands into the computer, he tried one of Stephanie's web addresses. The connection to the site went through with lightning speed.

"That was fast!" Stephanie exclaimed.

"Now—want to have some fun?" Ted asked. He raised his eyebrows mischievously.

"Uh—sure. What are you going to do?" Stephanie asked. She leaned closer to the screen.

"You'll see." Ted typed in another address and the web browser connected . . . to a teen chat room.

"These guys are great, and the chat is totally casual," Ted explained.

Stephanie had never been part of a chat room before, but she'd always wanted to try it out. She watched while Ted dove into the discussion using her screen name, Stepper.

> JuJuSweet: Hi, Stepper. Welcome to teen talk!
> Stepper: Hi. What's everyone chatting about today?
> DogBone8: General stuff.
> Stepper: General who? Washington?

Stephanie laughed out loud when Ted typed his response. As usual, Ted was totally funny.

A response blinked up on the screen.

> JuJuSweet: LOL, Stepper.

Together Stephanie and Ted continued to chat with JuJuSweet, DogBone8, and the other kids in the chat room. Stephanie couldn't believe how cool Ted was on-line. Within

minutes he was controlling the whole chat—
everyone in the room wanted to talk to him.

Ted is completely awesome, Stephanie thought.
*Whichever girl he asks to the picnic is really, really
lucky.*

MICHELLE

Chapter
5

Michelle flipped absently through the TV channels. She sighed. There was nothing on.

She glanced up the stairs when she heard the sound of Stephanie laughing.

Excellent, she thought. *Stephanie and Ted are having fun together.* As far as Michelle was concerned, that was a good sign. *Maybe now Ted will loosen up and ask Stephanie to the picnic.*

Michelle turned off the TV and slumped on the couch. Playing Cupid was totally worthwhile—but right now, she felt bored.

For a moment she thought about reading a

book. But what she really wanted to do was play her new game. She was so close to getting to the third level!

Michelle picked up her CD-ROM from the coffee table. She glanced over her shoulder toward the study.

Dad's computer is just sitting in there doing nothing, she thought. *It wouldn't hurt anything if I used it for just a few minutes, right?*

Michelle's father and Aunt Becky were on assignment for Wake Up, San Francisco, the morning talk show they hosted together. They wouldn't be home until late Monday afternoon. Joey and Uncle Jesse were still at the park with the twins, and D.J. was in class at college.

If she used the computer now, she could get to the third level and be out of the office before anyone even knew.

Michelle crept to the stairs and listened. Stephanie and Ted were still laughing and talking—totally occupied. *What can go wrong?* she asked herself. She opened the study door and walked inside.

Michelle settled into her dad's big leather

desk chair and turned on the computer. Except for a few different program icons on the screen, everything looked the same as it did on her computer upstairs.

Michelle slipped her game CD into the player and hit RUN. The machine whirred and installed the game.

"I'll quit right after I reach the third level," Michelle promised herself. She resumed playing where she had left off.

Soon she had defeated the monster dog. Two hours later she found herself ready to jump to the fourth level.

"All right!" Michelle cheered. "I rule this game." She punched a fist in the air.

Whoops, she thought when she caught sight of the clock on the wall. *I've been playing on Dad's computer for a really long time.*

She heard the front door open—and Nicky and Alex's voices!

Uh-oh. Uncle Jesse and Joey are home from the park with the twins, she realized. *If they see me in here, I'm busted!*

She jumped up, her fingers accidentally

brushing some of the keys on the keyboard. She grabbed the mouse, and clicked on the word QUIT.

The computer screen flickered and went black.

Michelle blinked. *Wait a minute—what was going on? The game was supposed to close with a burst of magical sparkles. Then the regular screen was supposed to return.*

Instead this screen was—black.

Something was very, very wrong.

Michelle heard footsteps approaching. She jumped up and dashed out of the study, closing the door behind her.

Joey came whistling into the living room with the mail. "Hi, Michelle," he greeted her.

"Hi." Michelle smiled and planted herself in front of the study door. Joey began to walk toward it.

"I'm going to put your dad's mail on his desk, okay?" Joey tried to move around her.

Michelle's heart skipped a beat. She threw her hands up and scooted sideways. "Uh—

we usually leave Dad's mail on the front hall table."

"And your dad usually comes home to pick it up," Joey explained. "But he won't be back until Monday, and I don't want it to get lost."

"You know what? You're right. Why don't I take that for you?" Michelle held out her hand.

Joey squinted at her. "Michelle, is there something behind this door that you don't want me to see?" he asked.

"No!" Michelle said. "It's just that you—you look tired, and I figured I'd do something nice for you."

Joey nodded. "Well . . . I have been chasing two four-year-old twins around the park for the last two hours. But that doesn't mean I can't—"

"Where are the twins?" Michelle interrupted.

"Jesse is giving them a nap." Joey yawned.

"Maybe you should take a nap, too." Michelle took her father's mail from Joey's hand. "I'm only nine and *I* can't keep up with Alex and Nicky. *You* must be exhausted."

Joey yawned again. "Actually, that's not such a bad idea. I think I will take a nap before dinner. Thanks for handling the mail, Michelle."

"No problemo," she answered.

Michelle waited until she heard Joey close the door to his bedroom in the basement. Then she tore back into the study. She threw the mail on her dad's desk and studied the computer screen—still blank.

She touched the power switch on the monitor, turning it off—then on again, but nothing changed.

Oh, no! What if I broke the computer? Michelle worried. *When Dad finds out what happened, he's going to ground me for the rest of my life!*

She started to take her game CD out of the computer, when she heard Stephanie and Ted at the top of the stairs.

"Thanks for everything, Ted," Stephanie said. "I really had fun on-line. *You* are a funny guy."

Michelle tiptoed to the study door and peeked out. *Ted,* she thought. *If anyone can help me with this problem, Ted can.*

"Thanks! Bye, Stephanie." Ted waved and hurried down the stairs.

Stephanie walked back toward the bedroom.

"Psssst. Ted!" Michelle whispered.

Ted glanced over and saw Michelle behind the study door. "Michelle, what—" he began to say.

"Shh!" Michelle put her finger to her lips and waved him into the study. "I'm in big trouble, and you're the only one who can save me," she told him.

Ted squatted down and frowned with concern. "What's up?"

Michelle quickly explained about the blank computer screen. "I didn't do anything differently than I do upstairs—honest—but the screen just went blank!" She paced the study floor. "If my dad finds out I broke his computer, he will be so incredibly mad. I'm not supposed to be using it."

Ted smiled and placed a hand on Michelle's shoulder to reassure her. "Let's have a look." He plopped down in Danny's chair.

Michelle crossed her fingers as Ted pressed different buttons on the computer. It began making a whirring noise.

Please let it be okay, she thought. *It has to be okay!*

The screen flickered. Three words appeared.

No disk present.

Ted sighed. "Uh-oh. That's what I was afraid of. The hard drive is shot, Michelle."

"Shot?" she cried. "*Shot?*" Michelle tried to keep her lower lip from trembling. "I *did* break it!" she moaned. "What am I going to do now?"

"Don't worry." Ted took her CD out of the drive and turned off the computer. "I think I can help."

"How?" Michelle sniffled.

"Well, your dad's files aren't totally lost, for one thing." Ted pointed to a small square box on top of the desk. "See that? That's a backup drive. Your dad has copies of everything on his computer in there."

"Uh-huh." Maybe Michelle didn't completely

48

understand, but if her dad's files were safe, that was good.

"If I install a new hard drive, I can transfer all your dad's files back onto the computer in a couple of hours." Ted grinned. "Cool, huh?"

"Yeah, except for one thing." Michelle bit her lip. "Where am I going to get a new hard drive? I can't buy one! I spent all my money on my game!"

Ted leaned forward. "How about if we make a deal?" he asked in a low voice.

"A deal? Sure!" Michelle exclaimed. "Whatever you want, Ted. Name it!"

"I can handle the cost of the new hard drive"—Ted glanced down at the carpet—"if you'll help me get a date with Stephanie."

Michelle stared at Ted for a moment. Was he serious?

"You know, I kind of like Stephanie," Ted admitted.

"Yeah, I noticed," Michelle said.

"And I want to ask her to go to the class picnic with me," he continued, "but I'm afraid she'll say no."

He stared seriously at Michelle. "You're her sister. You know her better than anyone. I'm sure that you can tell me the best way to get Stephanie to like me."

This deal is too good to be true, Michelle thought. *I was trying to get Stephanie and Ted to go out together anyway.*

"Well, first of all," Michelle started, "if you like Stephanie, why don't you just ask her to the picnic? You could march upstairs and do it right now!"

"No way." Ted's face grew pale. "I have to make her like me first."

"But she already likes you," Michelle pointed out. "She walks home with you after school, and she always laughs when you're around."

"That's true, but she needs to like me as more than a friend," Ted explained. "She has to think I'm cool. That's why I need your help."

Michelle paused. She suddenly had a brilliant idea. "What if you sent Stephanie a cool e-mail?" she suggested.

Ted's expression brightened. "Yeah, I'm really good at e-mail. I'll write a message tomorrow." He paused. "But what if she doesn't like it? I'll look really dumb for sending it."

Michelle sighed. Why did older kids have to make everything so complicated? "Well, what if you sent the e-mail without signing your name?" she suggested.

"Go on," Ted prodded.

"You could write her a letter—or a whole bunch of letters—and sign them 'from a secret admirer' or something," Michelle said. "*Then* we could see how she likes them and . . ."

"And then, depending on what Stephanie says about them, I can decide whether or not I want to tell her they're from me," Ted said, finishing Michelle's thought.

"Right." Michelle beamed.

"Excellent!" Ted jumped up from his seat. "Why didn't I think of that myself? You're the best, Michelle—and we've got a deal."

Michelle held out her hand, and the two of them shook on it. She felt *so* much better—Ted wouldn't let her down. Her dad's computer would be fixed by the time he returned from his trip.

And she wouldn't let Ted down, either.

Stephanie would never be able to resist a secret admirer who sent romantic e-mails. It was a foolproof plan. What could possibly go wrong?

STEPHANIE

Chapter 6

Stephanie spent a lot of the weekend and most of Monday printing out information about space colonies and working on her paper.

The whole concept of huge, contained cities in orbit was pretty amazing. Stephanie found that she was much more enthusiastic about the paper than she had been at first. *Ted's space-craziness must be catching*, she thought with a chuckle. She'd have to remember to give him a really big thank-you when this was all over.

It was almost four o'clock on Monday when Stephanie printed out the last article. She decided to check her e-mail while she waited.

Stephanie clicked on the mail icon on her Internet program. There was only one message in her mailbox. She didn't recognize the sender's address—TB03. But the title of the message had her name in it. *It must be from someone I know,* she reasoned.

She clicked the mouse and opened up the message.

"Whoa!" she gasped. As she read the e-mail, a warm flush crept up her neck.

Dear Stephanie,

Even though it's hard for me to tell you in person, I want you to know that I really like you. A LOT!

A Secret Admirer

Stephanie's heart did a flip-flop. "This is—this is *too* cool!" she said. A letter from a secret admirer!

But who is he? Stephanie wondered. She

studied his e-mail address—TB03. *Who could that be?*

The letters and numbers in an e-mail address usually stood for something. If she could figure out what *these* stood for then she'd know who sent the e-mail.

Stephanie clicked the PRINT icon. *I need backup on this,* she decided. She grabbed the message from the printer and rushed to the phone. She called Allie first, then got Darcy on the line using her three-way calling. "You both have to meet me at Pizza Palace in the mall right away," she told her friends.

"Steph, is everything all right?" Allie asked.

"Yeah," Darcy put in. "You sound like you're out of breath or something."

"Everything's fine. In fact, I have news that is totally fantastic. But I have to see you to tell you about it."

"Hold on a second," Darcy said. "I need to ask permission."

Stephanie held on while both Darcy and Allie spoke to their parents.

"No problem," Allie reported.

"Same here!" Darcy said. "My mom can even pick us all up and bring us home again."

"Great. If I can't get permission to meet you, I'll call you right back. Otherwise, I'll see you in fifteen minutes," Stephanie said. She hung up just as Michelle strolled into the room.

"Are you done with the computer yet, Stephanie?" Michelle asked as she walked toward the desk with her game CD.

"Almost." Stephanie intercepted Michelle before she reached the computer. She didn't want anyone but her best friends to know about her romantic e-mail—at least until she knew who had sent it. "Give me one more minute."

"What's that?" Michelle leaned to the side to look around Stephanie at the screen.

"Nothing." Stephanie closed the e-mail window. She folded the note in her hand and tucked it into her shoulder bag. "Okay, Michelle. The computer's all yours."

"Thanks," Michelle said.

Stephanie picked up her student directory, which contained the names, addresses, and phone numbers of every person at John Muir Middle School, and put that in her bag with the note.

"Where are you going?" Michelle asked.

"As long as Uncle Jesse or Joey says it's okay, I'm meeting Allie and Darcy at the Pizza Palace. I'll be back in time for dinner." Stephanie slung her bag over her shoulder and raced out of the room.

This is so exciting! Stephanie thought. A secret admirer—just in time for the class picnic. It was the absolute best news ever!

"Okay, what's up?" Darcy said as she slipped into the corner booth at Pizza Palace. She stared at Stephanie with her intense brown eyes. Allie slid into the booth beside her.

As usual, the Pizza Palace was packed with kids around Stephanie's age. The latest hit song by the Wallclimbers blared from the jukebox, and the staff was busy running pizza and sodas to the customers.

A waitress approached to take their order.

Stephanie, Darcy, and Allie requested a soda each and an order of mozzarella sticks to share.

Stephanie smiled at her friends. She could tell that they were completely bursting to hear what was going on.

"Spill," Allie said when the waitress had left. "What's the deal, Stephanie?"

Stephanie took a deep breath and handed over the printed e-mail message. "Read this!"

Both girls' eyes grew bigger as they scanned the paper.

"Whoa! Totally cool." Darcy sat back, grinning. "Who *is* this guy?"

"I don't know." Stephanie shrugged. "I was hoping you could help me figure it out." She pointed at the top of the paper. "Maybe there's a clue about my secret admirer in his screen name."

"Hmmm." Allie placed the paper faceup on the table and studied it, her chin propped up in her hand. "TB could be someone's initials," she offered.

"That's what I thought, too," Stephanie

said. She took a pen and her student directory out of her bag.

"Excellent!" Darcy grabbed the directory. "I'll look up everyone with the initials T.B. You take notes."

Stephanie and Allie paid close attention as Darcy started to read. "Baldwin, Tina; Babcock, Trisha; Bappas, Tommy." She paused.

"Hmmm. Think it could be Tommy?" Allie asked.

"No way." Stephanie shook her head. "Everyone knows Tommy likes Jennifer Grant."

Darcy glanced down at the book again. She gasped. "No—it can't be!"

"What?" Stephanie and Allie asked at the same time.

"Barnes!" Darcy nearly shouted. "Stephanie, what if the guy who wrote you that e-mail . . . is Todd Barnes?"

Stephanie stared at her friends, stunned. *Todd Barnes?* She wrote his name on the e-mail paper and circled it.

"Of course!" Allie cheered. "T.B.! Todd Barnes! It's him—I know it is!"

Stephanie's mind raced. Could the cutest, most popular boy in the eighth grade have a crush on her? Even after the chocolate-milk scene in the cafeteria the other day?

No way. It was too wild to believe.

Her heart thumped against her rib cage. "Wait—let's not jump to conclusions," she said. "I mean, there are lots of people with those initials," she paused. "And what about the '03' part? How does that fit in?"

"Oh my gosh! *That* just cinches it." Darcy smiled broadly. She folded her arms across her chest. "Anyone know what Todd's basketball team number is?"

Stephanie swallowed hard. "Zero three?" she guessed.

Darcy nodded, and the three girls let out a squeal.

"That's it! TB03!" Allie bounced in her seat. "Todd Barnes likes Stephanie!"

"Todd Barnes likes who?" Paula Warner approached the table. Her auburn hair was pulled into a high ponytail, and she was wearing her cheerleading uniform.

She must have come to the Pizza Palace straight from practice, Stephanie figured.

She didn't want to tell Paula the news, because she didn't want to spread a rumor she wasn't exactly sure was true. Especially if the rumor was about herself!

"No one," she answered.

"Todd Barnes likes Stephanie," Allie announced at the same time.

Paula's mouth fell open. "No way!"

"See for yourself." Darcy reached for the e-mail. Stephanie tried to stop her, but she was too late. Paula took the paper and began to read.

Paula frowned. "How do you know this is from Todd?" she asked.

"His e-mail address." Allie tapped the top of the piece of paper. "It's a combination of his initials and his basketball team number."

"Hey, you're right!" Paula handed the paper back. "Wow, Stephanie. You are *so* lucky."

"Yeah, *maybe* I am," Stephanie responded.

Paula hurried away. Stephanie's eyes followed her back to her table. When Paula sat down, she started talking excitedly and pointing at Stephanie.

"Oh, no," Stephanie groaned. "Paula's telling everyone at her table that Todd Barnes likes me!"

"So?" Allie asked.

"*So*, we're just guessing Todd sent the e-mail. We shouldn't have told anyone else. Not yet, anyway."

Darcy rolled her eyes. "Please. Who else could TB03 possibly be?"

Good question, Stephanie thought. *But what if he is someone else? What if we're wrong? What if TB03 isn't Todd Barnes at all?*

MICHELLE

Chapter
7

Michelle opened the front door before Ted had a chance to knock. She had called him as soon as Stephanie left for the Pizza Palace. "Come on in," Michelle said to him. "You're not going to believe this."

"Is it good news or bad?" Ted asked. He followed Michelle into her dad's study.

"Great news." Michelle felt as if she were going to burst with excitement.

"Awesome!" Ted smiled. "But first, I have some not-so-good news for you." He sat down in Michelle's dad's high-backed desk chair. "The new hard drive I got for your dad's computer won't be here until Friday."

"Friday!" Michelle pushed the study door closed. "What am I going to do till then? My dad will be home *tonight,* and he uses this computer all the time!"

"I'm sorry, but I had to order it from an on-line company. It takes a few days to deliver anything."

Michelle could tell Ted was really disappointed about the news, but it wasn't his fault she was in trouble. *He shouldn't feel guilty for trying to help me,* she thought.

"That's okay, Ted," Michelle said. "If I hadn't broken the hard drive in the first place, I wouldn't *need* a new one."

"You didn't break it, Michelle," Ted told her. "The hard drive just happened to fry out while you were using the computer."

"Yeah, well. I'll just have to keep my dad from finding that out until you fix it." Michelle tapped her foot, thinking, *how am I going to do that?*

Ted stared at the floor, twisting the swivel

chair back and forth. "So—uh—did Stephanie get my e-mail?"

"Yes. *That's* why I called you." Michelle put her own troubles aside to give Ted the good news.

Ted's face scrunched up. "What did she say?"

"She didn't *say* anything." Michelle sat in the extra chair beside the desk. "She wouldn't even let me see it. She just printed it out and took it to the Pizza Palace to show her friends."

"Her *friends!*" Ted sagged. "Oh, man. That's totally embarrassing. Now they'll all think I'm a supernerd."

Michelle shook her head. "Stephanie wouldn't let Darcy and Allie see your message if she thought it was embarrassing. Besides, she was totally excited about it. She was grinning from ear to ear when she left here."

"Are you sure?" Ted asked.

"Cross my heart." Michelle drew an *x* with her fingers on her chest. "You should send her a message every day," she suggested. "That will get her to really like you."

"*Every day?*" Ted frowned. "For how long?"

"Until *after* we move to step two," Michelle said.

"Step two?" Ted asked.

Michelle grabbed a copy of her favorite teen magazine, *Daisy*, from the top of the desk. She handed it to Ted.

Daisy was full of pictures of famous boys. Some were musicians, some were on TV or in the movies, but Michelle knew that Stephanie thought all of them were cute.

"If you really want Stephanie to go to the picnic with you, you should get your hair cut like one of these guys." She paused. "And maybe get an outfit like them, too."

"I don't know," Ted frowned as he paged through the book. "I kind of like my style. It's comfortable."

Michelle put her hands on Ted's shoulders. She spoke in a very serious voice. "Ted, lots and lots of girls, including Stephanie, like *these* styles." She pointed at the magazine. "It can't hurt to try one just for a little while can it?"

"I guess not." Ted sighed. "My mom could take us to the mall on Wednesday after school."

"Super!" Michelle beamed. "Between your e-mails and your new look, Stephanie will be *dying* to go to the picnic with you."

"Yeah," Ted said. "As long as she doesn't end up going with someone else."

At that moment the study door opened, and Danny stepped inside. Michelle's heart lurched. "Dad! You're home—early!"

"Hi, Michelle! Hi, Ted!" Danny greeted them. He dropped his briefcase by the study door and gave Michelle a hug. "What are you guys doing in here?" he asked.

Michelle glanced at Ted. He was frozen— too shocked to speak.

"We're just, uh—talking," Michelle said. "About a special surprise for Stephanie!"

"Well, that's sweet," Danny responded. He picked up his mail from the desk. "Would you two mind talking in the living room, though? I have to type up some notes on my computer."

"No," Michelle said, panicking. "You can't! I mean, *we can't*—talk in the living room. Stephanie could come home any minute. She might hear us."

Danny nodded. "All right. I'm going to change my clothes in the meantime, but don't be too long, okay?"

"Okay." Michelle forced a fake smile. Danny left the study and headed upstairs.

Michelle was safe, but only for a little while.

"I'm really sorry I can't get the hard drive sooner, Michelle." Ted jumped up and headed for the front door.

"Just get it as soon as you can," Michelle instructed. "I'll try to keep my dad away from the computer until then." She waved good-bye and closed the front door behind Ted.

Soon Danny returned to the living room and headed for the study.

Yikes! Now what do I do? Michelle dashed into the study after him. "Uh—how was your trip, Dad?" she asked.

"Great." Danny set his briefcase on the desk and opened it. "Becky and I were reporting from the San Diego Zoo. The whole family would have loved it. We should really go there sometime."

"That would be great," Michelle replied.

Danny reached for the computer's ON button.

"Dad!" Michelle yelled a little too loudly. "I have to tell you all about my new computer game."

Danny sat back in his chair. "Oh, right. How is 'Marla's Magical Mystery,' anyway?"

"It's great!" Michelle cheered. "I'm already on the fifth level." An idea flashed into her mind. "Why don't you come upstairs and play a round with me?"

"Sure." Danny agreed. "After I get these notes on file and e-mail them to my computer at the studio."

"But—" Michelle's mind raced. "But I've hardly seen you *all week!*"

Danny's expression grew serious. "I *have* been really busy. And we haven't been spending much time together lately, have we?"

Michelle shook her head. It was true, her

dad really had been too busy to hang out with her lately.

Danny grinned. "All right, Michelle, you win. No more work today. We'll play your game for a while before dinner. Then we'll rent a movie afterward. How does that sound?"

"Fantastic!" Michelle gave a little leap of joy. She was really happy that her father would be spending time with her, but there was a bonus—a whole evening without worrying about the computer.

Now, she thought, *all I have to do is figure out how to keep Dad away from his study for a few more days!*

Chapter
8

Look at this." Stephanie handed Allie the e-mail she had received before leaving for school Tuesday morning.

"*Another* message from TB03?" Darcy asked. She stuffed the books for her afternoon classes in her locker and slammed it closed.

Allie's eyes scanned the page. "Yep, and this one's even better than the first. Listen—"

"Allie, no." Stephanie looked up and down the corridor to make sure nobody else was paying attention.

"Relax, Stephanie. No one will hear." Allie

continued in a whisper. " 'Dear Stephanie, I think you're the prettiest girl in school—' "

"Too much!" Darcy interrupted with a muffled giggle.

" 'And I'm watching you from afar. With all my heart, TB03.' " Allie sighed as she gave the paper back to Stephanie. "Who would have thought Todd Barnes was so romantic?"

"Not me, that's for sure." Darcy glanced at the paper over Stephanie's shoulder.

Stephanie had to agree. It was amazing that superjock Todd had a sensitive side.

Popularity, good looks, and a mushy side— when you put it all together, Todd Barnes had the makings for the absolute best boyfriend ever.

"Hi, Stephanie!" Melinda Burns grinned and waved as she walked by. "How's it going?"

"Okay," Stephanie responded.

Ever since Paula told the world about Stephanie's e-mail, she'd become the most popular girl in school. Suddenly everyone in the eighth grade was treating her like they'd been friends for years.

"Too bad we're not electing the class president right now," Darcy teased. "You'd win, Stephanie."

"Maybe," Stephanie said.

Allie gasped. "There he is!"

Stephanie glanced down the hall and saw Todd Barnes talking with one of his teammates several feet away. He wore jeans and a blue, open-necked shirt, which highlighted his aqua-colored eyes.

Stephanie turned back to her friends. "What should I do?" she asked.

"Nothing!" Darcy cautioned. "Let Todd make the first move."

Stephanie nodded and stared straight into her locker.

"What's he doing?" she asked after a long, awkward minute passed.

"Talking to John Hart," Darcy reported.

Stephanie couldn't help it. She looked over her shoulder again. Todd turned away from his teammate to glance toward her.

"He's looking at you, Stephanie," Allie said, speaking through the smile she had plastered on her face.

"What if he comes over here? What will I say?" Stephanie wondered, staring into her locker once again.

"Looks like you don't have to worry about that just yet," Darcy told her. "Todd's walking away."

Stephanie let out her breath in a *whoosh*. She was relieved, but also disappointed.

What was the deal? she wondered. Did Todd like her or not? And if he really did send those e-mails, then why didn't he come over to talk to her?

"Maybe he's shy," Darcy suggested at lunch in the cafeteria. "I mean, why else would anyone sign a love letter anonymously?"

Stephanie couldn't believe it—after two amazingly sweet e-mails, Todd still hadn't come over to talk to her. He sat across the way, at his regular lunch table, pretending that absolutely nothing was going on between them.

Stephanie frowned. "Have you seen Todd on the basketball court? He doesn't exactly seem like the shy type."

Darcy shrugged. "Basketball and dating are two different things."

"Maybe . . ." Stephanie considered the point.

"You have to do something," Allie insisted. "It would be terrible if you and Todd didn't get together because both of you waited too long to make the first move."

"Right," Darcy agreed.

"Hi-ho, Stephanie!" Ted appeared at the end of the table. He was wearing a brown plaid shirt and brown corduroy pants.

If anyone else were wearing that outfit, Stephanie thought, *I'd gently suggest a change of wardrobe. But on Ted the clothes are just— well—Ted.*

He set a paper lunch bag down and brushed his hair off his forehead. "Hi, Darcy. Hi, Allie. Mind if I sit with you guys?"

Stephanie smiled. "Go right ahead."

Ted sat down and began to chat, but Stephanie barely heard a word. Her attention was riveted on Todd's table.

"So, what's for lunch?" Darcy asked, peeking into Ted's brown bag.

He blushed. "You're going to think it's totally weird."

"No way," Allie said, encouraging him. "Tell us!"

"It's a sandwich—two of them, actually. My favorite kind—peanut butter and Marshmallow Fluff."

Ted took the sandwiches out of his bag. Stephanie turned, still a little distracted. "Hey, that's one of my favorite sandwiches, too," she said.

"Really?" Ted asked.

"Yeah, except I don't get to have them much. My dad says Marshmallow Fluff has too much sugar. But when Joey does the grocery shopping, I'm in fluff heaven!"

"If you want, you can have one of my sandwiches," Ted offered.

All right! Stephanie thought. For a second she nearly took Ted up on the offer. Then she remembered Todd. She didn't want to end up talking to him with peanut butter breath.

"Um—no, thanks." She shook her head.

"Okay." Ted rose from his place. "I'm going to get a soda. Be back in a second."

As he walked off toward the vending machine, Stephanie caught a flutter of movement. Out of the corner of her eye, Stephanie saw two of Todd's friends leaving their table. There was a ton of space available—ready for the taking.

Stephanie stood and picked up her tray. "I've had it," she announced to her friends. "If Todd's too shy to come to me, I'll just have to go to him!"

Smiling her biggest and brightest smile, Stephanie headed toward Todd's table.

STEPHANIE

Chapter
9

Stephanie stopped by the empty chair across from Todd, and smiled. "Hi," she said simply.

Todd looked up. He gave a slight nod. Two of his teammates, John and Ty, barely glanced at her.

For a few horrible seconds, Stephanie thought *nobody* was going to talk to her.

Then she realized not only was Todd silent, but he had lowered his gaze. He shifted in his seat like he was uncomfortable.

I bet he's afraid I'll say something about his

romantic notes in front of his friends, Stephanie thought.

Of course, she would never do anything to embarrass Todd, but Todd didn't know that.

"Hey, Stephanie. Have a seat," Melinda Burns said. She pushed her long black hair off her shoulders and patted the back of an empty chair—the chair directly across from Todd.

"Thanks." Stephanie set down her tray and slid into the seat. Shivers ran up and down her spine. *She* was having lunch at *Todd Barnes's* table. She was so close to him, she could almost touch him.

Stephanie glanced back at her friends. Darcy and Allie gave her two enthusiastic thumbs-up signs.

"Hey, Stephanie." Melinda tapped her on the shoulder. "Paula told me that if I saw you, I should let you know that tryouts for the cheerleading squad are a week from tomorrow—after school in the gym."

"Tryouts?" Stephanie asked, confused.

"Didn't you hear? Everyone on the team totally wants you to join," Melinda explained.

Stephanie frowned. She had never considered trying out for cheerleading before. It never seemed quite her speed. And none of her friends were—

"You're trying out for cheerleading?" a boy's voice broke through her thoughts.

Stephanie turned and saw Todd looking directly at her. "That's totally cool," he said.

"Really?" Stephanie asked.

Todd nodded.

"Well, then—yeah," Stephanie announced. "I guess I am trying out."

All right! She and Todd were finally having a conversation.

"Think fast," John said. He threw a wadded-up straw wrapper at Todd.

Todd ducked. The paper sailed over his head and landed on the next table—right in someone's soda.

Yuck! Stephanie thought.

"Man! I can't believe I missed." John frowned and lifted his milk carton.

"Nice aim—and you call yourself a basketball player?" Todd teased.

John took a swig of milk. "I'm a better shot than you are."

Melinda rolled her eyes. "Here we go," she said to Stephanie. "These guys will never grow up."

"Huh?" Stephanie asked, confused.

"Come on, Todd." John taunted. He held his half-full milk carton as if it were a basketball and eyed the trash container against the wall. "Best shot wins. Dare you."

"You're on." Todd grabbed his milk carton. "Three, two, one!" Both boys heaved their milk cartons at the pail.

Stephanie cringed as one of the cartons struck the edge. Milk sprayed everywhere, dousing a couple of kids who happened to be passing by. When the container hit the floor, the rest of the milk spilled out into a big white puddle.

John gave Todd a high five. "You the man!" John cheered. "Two points for Todd!"

How rude, Stephanie thought. *They didn't even apologize to the people they splashed.*

How could supercool, superromantic Todd be acting so childishly?

Disturbed, Stephanie glanced over her shoulder toward her table. Allie and Darcy were speaking excitedly to each other, but Ted was watching her.

He looks disappointed, Stephanie thought. *Like he can't believe I'm sitting here while Todd and his friends are acting like idiots.*

Stephanie sighed. *The funny thing is*, she thought, *neither can I.*

Stephanie thought the lunch hour would never end. She and Todd didn't say anything more to each other. When the bell rang, Allie and Darcy caught her in the hall.

"That was too much." Allie's eyes sparkled.

"You actually ate lunch with Todd Barnes," Darcy said, giving Stephanie a wide grin.

"You are so lucky, Stephanie," Allie added.

"Not *that* lucky," Stephanie said. She had to be honest with her best friends. "Todd acted as if I wasn't even there."

"Are you kidding?" Darcy looked surprised. "When Todd dunked that milk carton, he was obviously showing off for *you!*"

"He was?" Stephanie thought for a moment. "Then why didn't he talk to me? I mean, he hardly said anything."

Allie and Darcy exchanged glances.

"Because John was sitting right there," Darcy explained.

"Yeah." Allie nodded in agreement. "Todd probably doesn't want his basketball buddies to know he's a hopeless romantic."

Stephanie frowned. *That makes sense. And it's not like Todd totally ignored me*, she thought.

Besides, Todd's e-mails told her everything he was too shy to talk about in person.

He'd keep sending the e-mails, and eventually he'd stop being embarrassed about her in front of his friends.

I'll just have to be patient—and available for the picnic—until Todd gets over it, Stephanie vowed.

Chapter
10

Michelle sat on her bed doing her homework that night while Stephanie worked on the computer.

Michelle tapped her pencil on her bottom lip, staring at the page. It was taking her twice as long as usual to finish, because her mind kept wandering.

Her dad was out for the evening, so she was sure he wouldn't be using the broken computer. But she couldn't help wondering about the situation between Ted and Stephanie.

Stephanie had been totally excited after getting Ted's second e-mail message that morning, but she didn't seem very happy tonight. Had something gone wrong?

"Are you mad about something, Stephanie?" Michelle asked. "You've been awfully quiet."

"No." Stephanie glanced at her with a tight smile. "I'm just busy."

Why don't I believe you? Michelle frowned.

One thing was certain—she had to find out what was going on.

"The class picnic is Saturday. Do you have a date yet?" Michelle asked.

Stephanie shook her head. "No, but there's still plenty of time for Todd to ask me. At least, that's what I keep telling myself."

"Todd!" Michelle blurted out the name. She cleared her throat. "I mean—Todd? Who's that?"

Stephanie seemed to think before answering. "A boy from school." She shrugged.

Michelle sagged with relief. Whew. Todd couldn't be anything like Stephanie's boyfriend if she was only calling him "a boy from school."

But if Ted didn't get over his shyness and get his behind in gear, Todd might become Stephanie's boyfriend!

Michelle finished her last two math problems and returned her books to her backpack. She glanced up and saw Stephanie set her schoolwork aside.

I bet she's going to check her e-mail, Michelle thought. *I hope Ted sent his next note!*

Michelle took her backpack to the door and glanced at the computer screen as she passed by. She saw the on-line name TB03 next to the only message listed in Stephanie's e-mail window.

Stephanie gave a little bounce of happiness in her chair when she saw the e-mail. She opened it and read it.

Michelle felt a smile spread across her face. She knew it! Her sister loved Ted's messages!

Ted had told Michelle earlier what he planned to write about. He said that when he sat with Stephanie in the cafeteria today, he wanted to tell her how much he liked her. But, because she was so pretty, she made him too nervous to say so in person, in front of all those people.

What girl *wouldn't* love that?

Stephanie sighed dreamily at the computer screen.

"What are you looking at, Steph?" Michelle couldn't help asking.

"Nothing!" Stephanie blocked the screen with her hand. She quickly hit the PRINT button on the e-mail program, and shut the computer screen off.

Michelle snickered to herself. Stephanie had no idea she already knew what was in the e-mail.

"Guess I'll go watch TV," she told her sister. "My homework's done."

"Uh—sure," Stephanie said, continuing to block Michelle's view of the now-blank computer screen.

Michelle padded down the stairs. She grabbed the cordless phone from the living room and settled down on the couch. Quickly she punched in Ted's number.

Ted must have been waiting by the phone because he picked up before the first ring ended. "Did she get it?" Ted asked.

"Yep," Michelle said. "And I could tell she just loved it."

"Great!" Ted exclaimed.

"I think it's safe now," Michelle told him. "I think it's time for you to tell Stephanie who sent the letters."

"I guess . . ." Ted replied. Michelle thought he sounded more anxious than usual.

"Hey, is something wrong?" Michelle asked.

"I don't know." Ted sighed. "Stephanie sat with Todd Barnes and some other guys on the basketball team during lunch today. What if she likes one of them? What if one of them already asked her to the picnic?"

"No problem," Michelle responded. "Stephanie may have been sitting with boys from the basketball team, but I happen to know for a *fact* that not one of them asked Stephanie to the class picnic."

"Really?" Ted's voice sounded brighter.

"Absolutely," Michelle assured him. "And after you get a haircut and some new clothes, and tell Stephanie you're her secret admirer, she'll be thrilled to go to the picnic—*with you*."

"I sure hope so." Ted paused. "Oh, by the way, the new hard drive for your dad's computer will be here Friday. I can install it and transfer your dad's files after school."

"Great! Thanks, Ted," Michelle cheered.

Before they said good-bye, Michelle told Ted she had permission to go to the mall with him the next day for his total makeover.

Ted promised her that he and his mom would pick her up at Fraser Elementary when school got out the next day.

After she hung up, Michelle reached for the remote and turned on the TV. Cool! A rerun of *Teen Times* was on! *Teen Times* was Michelle and Stephanie's favorite show—and this was one of the episodes she had missed.

Michelle paid close attention to the program. She wasn't sure how much time had passed, when the front door opened.

"Hi, Pumpkin!" Danny greeted her and walked in the door.

"Hey, Dad," Michelle answered, her gaze still fixed on the television.

Dad! her mind screamed. She turned in her

seat and saw her father walking toward the study.

No! She had to get him away from the computer, but how? She did the only thing she could think of. She filled her lungs with air—and let out a shriek.

"Michelle!" Danny rushed over. "What's wrong?"

Joey ran in from the kitchen holding a dishtowel. "Who's screaming? What happened?"

Good question, Michelle thought in a panic. *Why did I scream?*

An idea came to her. She jumped up so that she was now standing on the seat of the couch. "I-I saw a mouse!" she stuttered.

"In here?" Danny put his hands on Michelle's shoulders to comfort her. "No, honey. That's impossible."

Michelle knew that her father was right. He kept the place too neat—he cleaned in every nook and cranny. A mouse would have no place to hide with her dad around.

"A mouse?" Joey jumped onto the sofa

beside Michelle. "Where?" His gaze darted around the floor.

"It—it—uh—ran under the couch!" Michelle blurted out.

Danny glanced at Joey. "Why don't you take a look under there for Michelle?" he asked.

Joey raised an eyebrow. "Me? You mean get down on my hands and knees and *search* for a mouse? What if it attacks me?"

"Mice don't attack, Joey," Danny pointed out. "They run."

Joey quietly and carefully stepped off the couch. Then he dropped to all fours with the dishtowel still in his hand. He glanced up at Michelle. "I'm going in. Cover me!" he joked.

Michelle had to stifle a giggle as Joey carefully lifted the skirt of the couch to look under it.

"Aaaah!" Joey screamed. He fell back.

Michelle was startled. *There couldn't really be a mouse under the couch, could there?*

"False alarm!" Joey held up his hand. "Nobody panic—it's just a dust bunny."

Danny turned Michelle around to face him.

"Honey," he began. "I really don't think there's a mouse under that couch."

Michelle gulped. "You don't?" she asked.

"No. But just in case you're right, let's keep this news between the three of us. I don't want the whole family in a panic over a silly little pest."

"Okay, Dad," Michelle promised.

"It's dark under there," Joey interrupted, still peering under the couch. "I can't see anything."

"I'll get a flashlight." Danny went into the kitchen. When he returned, he had the flashlight and a plastic mixing bowl. He got down on his hands and knees and handed the bowl to Joey. "When the mouse comes out, try to trap it under the bowl," he instructed.

"Okay." Joey held the bowl upside down in both hands. "Ready when you are."

Danny turned on the flashlight, took a deep breath, then raised the skirt on the sofa again.

Joey leaned forward to pounce.

Danny reached under the couch. "There's nothing under here but this." He pulled out a white sock.

"That's mine." Joey took the sock and stuffed it into his pocket. "Sorry."

Danny breathed a sigh of relief. "Well, now that that's over, I'm going to the study to do some work."

"But the mouse could have run someplace else," Michelle insisted. She leaped off the couch and grabbed her father's hand. "You have to check my bedroom. You have to sit with me until I go to sleep. I don't want to wake up with a mouse sleeping on my head!"

"Okay." Danny said, giving in.

"Thanks, Dad." Michelle gave him her most winning smile. "You're the best."

Chapter 11

Stephanie hurried toward the cafeteria on Wednesday afternoon. As she turned the corner by the entrance she saw Todd coming toward her from the opposite direction.

He gave her a broad smile and waved. "Hi, Stephanie."

"Hi," she responded.

Todd glanced into the crowded cafeteria. Most of the eighth grade was already in the food line. He waved at John and Ty.

"Save me a seat at our table, okay?" Todd

9 4

asked. "It's so mobbed, we might not get one."

Save a seat at our *table?* Stephanie thought. We *might not get one?*

Awesome! Todd was finally starting to talk like a boy who liked her. Major break-through.

"Sure, Todd. No problem," she answered. She went straight to the table and sat down.

Stephanie watched as Todd cut into the line behind Ty and picked up a tray. She scanned the rest of the cafeteria while she waited for Todd to return. Allie and Darcy were talking together and didn't see her trying to get their attention.

Then Stephanie saw Ted Bailey in the middle of the food line. She smiled and waved when she caught his eye. Ted stopped and waved back with a grin.

By the time Todd returned and Stephanie got in the food line, the only thing left was spinach casserole. Yuck! Looked like she'd have to settle for an apple and a cinnamon crunch granola bar.

As she headed back with her lunch tray, she felt a twinge of irritation. Todd's tray was full of totally great stuff. Three slices of pizza, salad, and a pudding cup for dessert. It seemed weird that he would let her get stuck with the spinach casserole if he really liked her.

The table was packed with basketball players and a bunch of the cheerleaders—including Paula and Melinda. But Todd had saved the chair beside him, Stephanie noticed, for her! She sat down, and everyone greeted her like one of the gang.

"How are you doing, Stephanie?" Ty asked.

"Totally great," Stephanie answered.

"Hey, don't forget cheerleading tryouts next Wednesday," Paula reminded her.

"I just know you'll be great, Stephanie," Melinda added.

Todd nodded. "Stephanie would make a great cheerleader."

"Thanks." Stephanie beamed.

Amazing, she thought. Todd was coming out of his shell around her. And not only that—his friends liked her. At that moment life was almost too perfect.

The only thing that could make it more perfect is some time alone with Todd, Stephanie thought. Then I could get to know the real him—the one who wrote the e-mail.

Todd turned and spoke directly to Stephanie. "I'm going to the mall after school. Want to meet me?"

Stephanie blinked. *It's like he's reading my mind!* she thought.

She nodded. "I'd love to. What time?"

"The Game Arcade at four-thirty," Todd told her.

"I'll be there," Stephanie stated. She reached out for her milk. Whoops! Wait a minute—she'd forgotten to get one! "I'm going to grab a milk, Todd. Do you want anything?"

"I could use a soda," he said without hesitation.

"Me, too." Ty tipped his empty milk carton upside-down.

"Make that three." John grinned.

Wait a minute. Why do I suddenly feel like the team gopher? Stephanie thought.

She decided not to say anything. She didn't want to spoil the progress she was making with Todd. Instead she focused on the positive. *This afternoon I'm going to the mall with Todd Barnes—just the two of us!*

MICHELLE

Chapter
12

The whole day dragged for Michelle. She was too excited about going to the mall for Ted's big makeover to think about spelling and math. She was going to make Ted look supercool. Stephanie was going to flip out when she saw him!

Later that afternoon Michelle entered the mall with Ted and his mom. Mrs. Bailey had been waiting for her in the parking lot when school got out.

Stephanie doesn't know it yet, but Ted is her perfect match. After I'm done, she'll see it, too, Michelle vowed to herself.

"Where do we start?" Ted asked after his mom left to do her errands.

Michelle placed a finger on her chin and studied him for a moment. Ted shifted his weight and swept his hair out of his eyes. "I think we'd better get the new hairstyle first," Michelle said. "You don't need an appointment at Beauty Beat, but we might have to wait."

"You're taking me to a place called Beauty Beat?" Ted held up his hands. "Oh, no. No way. I don't want to be seen going into a girl's beauty salon!"

"But *everybody* who's cool goes there." Michelle planted her hands on her hips. "Even the boys. Come on, I'll show you."

Michelle started walking before Ted could argue. Just as they got to the shop, two high school boys walked out with what looked like new haircuts.

Ted shrugged with a sheepish smile. "Guess you were right, Michelle."

"Trust me, Ted," Michelle assured him. "I know what I'm doing."

"Well, I hope so—because Stephanie sat at Todd's table for lunch again today," Ted informed her.

"*Todd* isn't the secret admirer who writes the e-mails Stephanie's saving in her notebook. *You* are," she pointed out. "As soon as you tell Stephanie that, she'll see you in a whole new light."

With that, Michelle led Ted into Beauty Beat.

Emily Hawkins, the owner of the shop, was free to take Ted. Michelle was thrilled. Emily loved her young customers, and Michelle knew that she'd give Ted a hairstyle that was perfect for him.

"Let's see." Emily frowned and looked at Ted from all angles when he was seated in the chair.

Michelle cocked her head, too. Ted's hair was long and kind of flat. She was sure he wouldn't miss having to brush it out of his eyes all the time.

"Would you take off your glasses, Ted?" Emily asked.

"Sure." Ted removed his thick-framed glasses and squinted at the mirror.

Michelle stared at Ted, amazed. *Wow!* she thought. *Behind those glasses Ted has amazing green eyes! He should leave the glasses off more often.*

Emily picked up her scissors and smiled. "Get ready for a whole new look," she told Ted.

When she had finished styling his hair, Ted looked really great. His brown hair was short now, but not too short, and it was layered on top so it didn't lie flat. The long bangs were gone, and Emily spiked the front with a little mousse. Ted looked totally cool—until he put his glasses back on.

Michelle didn't say anything until they were out on the mall concourse. "Do you always have to wear your glasses?" she asked.

"If I want to see. Everything is fuzzy and my depth perception is shot when I don't wear them," Ted answered. "Why?"

"Well, the new hair looks great, but—" Michelle didn't want to hurt Ted's feelings, but she had to be honest. "You look a lot, uh— *better* without your glasses. Why don't you just try walking around without them?"

"All right." Ted took off the glasses and gave them to Michelle. He squinted, attempting to see her. "Maybe you'd better lead the way, Michelle. Everything's a little blurry."

"Okay. Next stop, Safari Closet," Michelle said. "They've got dynamite stuff for teens. At least, that's what Stephanie says."

"I'll take her word for it." Ted smiled. He moved his hand to brush back his bangs, then realized they weren't there. "Funny," he said with a grin. "It's been such a habit. I'll have to get used to my new no-bangs look."

The mall was busy and Michelle had to weave through the crowd. She tried to go slowly so Ted could follow her.

A poster in the movie theater window caught her eye. She stopped to glance at it just as the theater doors burst open. The afternoon movie crowd began streaming out. Michelle and Ted were pushed apart in the confusion.

"Michelle?" Ted called.

"Over here," Michelle answered. *Ted can't find me because I've got his glasses,* she realized.

"Michelle!" Ted called, his voice panicky as he was bumped and shoved by the crowd.

"Don't move, Ted!" Michelle yelled.

When the theater was finally empty, Michelle dashed over to Ted and handed him his glasses.

"On second thought," she told him, "maybe you should leave these on. It's probably safer if you can see what you're doing. Besides, Stephanie likes guys who look smart."

"Right," Ted muttered. "That's why she's hanging out with the basketball team instead of the Science Club."

Michelle frowned. Ted had a point, but she refused to be worried. She just knew her plan would work. It had to!

"Come on," she cheered. "Let's go get that new wardrobe so you can look smart *and* ultracool."

Michelle and Ted spent an hour going through all the racks in Safari Closet. They finally settled on three new outfits that were on sale: two pairs of cargo pants and a pair of black jeans to wear with a zippered polo, a velour v-neck shirt, and a funnel-neck pullover.

The last shirt was exactly like the kind that Stephanie's favorite band, the O-Boys, wore in their pictures in *Daisy* magazine.

Ted went into the changing rooms to try the first outfit. Once he had it on, he shuffled out of the changing area to show Michelle how he looked. His hands were shoved into his pockets, his shoulders were hunched, and his head hung low.

Michelle thought he looked totally uncomfortable, but totally stylish. "Wow!" she called to Ted. "You look amazing."

"Really?" Ted asked, sounding unsure.

"She's right," another voice said. Michelle turned and saw a salesperson approaching. "Those clothes are the absolute latest style. And they really suit you."

"You think so?" Ted turned to study himself in the mirror. He stood up a little straighter. A broad smile formed on his face. "Great! I'm going to try on the next outfit." He bolted for the changing room.

Ted is going to look totally sharp tomorrow, Michelle thought with satisfaction. She waited for Ted to go through the checkout line. All three outfits he tried on were great, so he decided to buy them all. He paid for the clothes with the money his mother had given him.

Ted glanced at his watch as he and Michelle headed out of Safari Closet. Michelle noticed that he was standing taller. Even his walk was different.

He's so much more confident now that he knows he looks good, Michelle realized. *In fact, he's so confident, Stephanie probably won't even recognize him when she sees him.*

"It's only four-forty, Michelle," Ted said. "We don't have to meet my mom for twenty minutes—and I've got ten dollars left over. So why don't we go to the Game Arcade?"

"Cool!" Michelle grinned. "I would love that!"

The Game Arcade was near the side exit where Michelle and Ted had agreed to meet Mrs. Bailey. Michelle hoped no one was playing 'Comet Countdown'—one of her favorite games. Maybe she and Ted could have a two-player showdown together.

The Game Arcade was a big hangout for all kinds of kids. Today it was busy, but not too crowded.

Excellent, Michelle thought. Just the way she liked it.

Michelle led Ted toward the video pinball machines at the rear of the arcade—and suddenly came to a halt.

She inhaled sharply—Stephanie! What was she doing here?

Stephanie was standing with three boys. Each of them wore a jacket that read "J.M.M.S. Basketball" on the back.

"What's wrong, Michelle?" Ted asked with a frown.

"Uh—nothing!" Michelle couldn't let Ted

see Stephanie with the boys from the basket-ball team! It would ruin his newfound confidence. Then he'd never get up the nerve to tell Stephanie that he was her secret admirer.

Michelle panicked when Ted started to look in Stephanie's direction.

Do something, she ordered herself. Michelle reached up and did the only thing she could think of. She whipped the glasses off Ted's face.

There, she thought. *Now he can't see anything!*

She gulped—*including the fact that Stephanie's coming right toward us!*

STEPHANIE

Chapter 13

Stephanie frowned. She had expected to find Todd waiting for her at the Game Arcade alone. He had been there, all right—except he had brought his teammates John, Ty, and Jack Kruger along with him.

The three of them had decided to have a video game showdown—without Stephanie.

Man, she thought, rolling her eyes. *Are these guys always competing? Can't they just hang out like normal people?*

Todd rubbed his hands on his jeans, then grabbed the controls. "Prepare to eat dust."

John and Jack edged in front of Stephanie, and each of them took his own set of controls. With a blast of music, the game started.

Great. Now she couldn't even see the game!

She sighed, remembering how she had day-dreamed all afternoon about how she and Todd would spend their time at the mall together.

She had been so sure they would get something to eat or see a movie—just the two of them.

I certainly didn't expect to be standing around twiddling my thumbs, she thought.

She turned and watched him—Mr. Popularity—concentrating on the screen. She decided it wouldn't hurt to cheer him on.

"You can do it, Todd," Stephanie said.

"Tell me about it. I've got these guys beaten—badly." Todd's eyes narrowed as he pushed the controls for turbo power.

Stephanie rolled her eyes. *Todd sure doesn't have a problem with confidence,* she thought. When the game was over, Todd was proved right. He finished several hundred points higher than Ty or John.

Stephanie quickly took advantage of the opening. "Wow! That was fantastic, Todd. But maybe you and I can do something else now. We could go get some pizza," she suggested. "Are you hungry?"

I sure am, Stephanie realized. *Especially after eating only an apple and a granola bar for lunch.*

Todd shook his head. "Nah, I want to stick around here some more."

"Okay. Well, we can always check out the CD store together when you're done," Stephanie tried again. "They're having a gigantic sale."

"Yeah, I guess," Todd responded. "If the guys want to." He turned his back on her as Ty started a new game.

Ugh. Todd is stuck to his friends like glue, Stephanie thought. *What's wrong with this picture?*

She came up with the answer immediately: The Todd Barnes she was getting to know in person was completely different from TB03—the Todd Barnes who wrote her those wonderful e-mails.

How can someone who acts the way Todd does

write notes that are so sweet and sensitive? she wondered.

Stephanie's stomach gave a growl. That was it, she decided. She *had* to get a candy bar from the vending machine across the court-yard.

Without a word, she moved toward the exit of the arcade. As she approached it, she did a double take.

Michelle! What was she doing here? And why was she with a totally cute stranger?

Stephanie watched, stunned, as Michelle and a boy about Stephanie's age laughed together. It looked as if they were playing a game of keep away. The boy was trying to grab something out of Michelle's hands.

"Michelle!" Stephanie hurried over to see what was going on.

Michelle stopped playing and turned toward Stephanie. "Uh—hi!" she responded.

The boy grabbed a pair of glasses from Michelle's hand and slipped them on.

Stephanie blinked. *Oh my gosh!* "Ted?" she asked. "Is that you?"

Ted smiled. "Hi, Stephanie," he said smoothly.

Stephanie squinted at her next door neighbor. Ted was much more recognizable with his thick-rimmed glasses, but there was something about him that looked . . . different. Stephanie couldn't quite put a finger on it.

"He got a haircut," Michelle offered. "And he—uh—asked me to come along with him to get it."

"It's fabulous, Ted." Stephanie complimented him. Inside she couldn't help thinking, *What a difference. He looks awesome!*

Then another thought occurred to her. *Wow! Whoever Ted was thinking about asking to the picnic is sure to say yes now. Ted's a total cutie.*

Stephanie frowned. *Why have I never noticed that before?* she wondered.

"We were about to play some games," Ted explained, pointing into the arcade. "We're waiting for my mom to finish shopping."

"Cool." Stephanie noticed that, so far, Ted hadn't stumbled over any of his words—and he hadn't nervously swept his hair back once.

113

Excellent. Ted was finally loosening up. Maybe his new haircut had given him confidence.

"It was nice of you to bring Michelle to the mall with you," Stephanie told Ted. "She loves the arcade. Right, Michelle?"

"Um—sure!" Michelle answered.

"Son, tell me, what's your favorite video game, Stephanie?" Ted asked.

"I like them all—but my favorites are the racing games," she told him.

"Me too!" Ted nodded. "Why don't you, Michelle, and I have a three-player game!"

"I'd love to!" Stephanie grinned. Playing *with* Ted and Michelle would be a lot more fun than *watching* Todd compete with his buddies.

"Sounds great," Michelle blurted out. "Except that we have to go." She grabbed Ted's sleeve and began dragging him toward the door of the arcade.

"Wait a minute," Ted protested. "I'm not ready to leave."

"Sorry, I just remembered something *really*

important we have to do!" Michelle said, tugging on his sleeve.

"Okay." Ted gave Stephanie a sheepish smile. "I'll see you later." He waved and allowed Michelle to haul him out of the arcade.

That was weird, Stephanie thought. *I usually have to drag Michelle away from the video games when we're in the mall. I wonder what was so important.*

"There you are." Todd came up behind Stephanie. "I wondered what happened to you."

"You did?" Stephanie asked, surprised.

Todd nodded. He glanced down the hallway toward Michelle and Ted. "Who were you talking to?" he asked. "That's not Ted-the-nerd-head is it?"

Stephanie stared at Todd, shocked. Could someone who had written so many nice things to her have really said something so nasty?

"He—He's not a nerd," she managed to argue.

115

"Whatever." Todd reached into his pocket and pulled out some quarters. He dropped them into Stephanie's hand. "Hey, you wouldn't mind getting me a soda from the vending machines across the courtyard, would you?"

Stephanie's fingers closed over the coins.

"Thanks, Stephanie. You're great." Todd smiled—then gave her hand a squeeze.

Still stunned, Stephanie trudged toward the vending machines across the main concourse. As she walked, her mind whirled.

The basketball player, or the e-mail writer, she thought. *Which one was the real Todd Barnes?*

STEPHANIE

Chapter
14

When the last bell rang on Thursday afternoon, Stephanie jogged to her locker. Darcy
and Allie were already there, gathering the
books they'd need for that night's homework.

Stephanie spun the combination on her lock
and opened the door.

"Steph, I have the greatest news!" Allie called
to her. "Guess who asked me to the picnic?"

Stephanie turned to face her friend. "Who?"
she asked.

"George Morriss!" Allie answered. Her eyes
were shining.

"He's the guy from the debate team that Allie likes," Darcy filled in.

"Wow!" Stephanie said. "That is so great. You must be psyched, Allie."

"I am," Allie answered. "And it's so great that we all have dates now."

"Uh—I wouldn't exactly say that yet." Stephanie frowned.

"What do you mean?" Darcy questioned. "Isn't Todd going to ask you to the picnic?"

"I thought so." Stephanie sighed. "But now he's got me completely confused!"

"Confused how?" Allie asked.

"Todd writes such wonderful things to me one minute—and acts like such a jerk the next," she explained.

She reviewed for her friends the series of events that happened after school the day before. She ended by telling them that when Todd finally asked her to play a video game with him, Ty and John were still there, cheering Todd on against Stephanie!

Then, that night, Stephanie had received an e-mail from TB03. His note talked about how nice it was to see Stephanie at the mall, even if they didn't get to spend much time with each other. He said he hoped to spend more time at the Game Arcade—just the two of them—sometime soon.

He also hinted that in the next day or two, he had something very important to ask her.

"Well, that sounds good!" Darcy interjected.

"Yeah, except that I haven't seen Todd all day. He didn't bother to tell me that he was having lunch with his coach and the rest of the basketball team in the gym today. So I sat at 'our usual table' waiting for someone who never showed up!"

"Todd probably just forgot to mention it," Allie offered.

"I guess." Stephanie sighed as she put the books she didn't need in her locker. "I just wish Todd would do something to show that he likes me! Something besides sending e-mails."

"Hey, Stephanie!" Todd's voice rang down the corridor.

Stephanie's heart jumped as she looked up and saw Todd coming toward her.

She couldn't be annoyed with him when he waved and smiled at her. *He's just so adorable!* Stephanie thought.

She closed her locker and slung her bag over her shoulder. "Hey, Todd," she said as casually as possible. "What's up?"

"I need directions to your house so I can pick you up Saturday," he said.

"Huh?" Puzzled, Stephanie frowned.

"For the class picnic," Todd explained.

"Oh!" Stephanie said, surprised.

This was certainly a weird way of asking her to be his date, but the bottom line was still the same. *Todd Barnes* did *want to go to the picnic with her!*

Stephanie pulled a pad and pen from her bag and wrote down her address and directions. "It's pretty easy to find," she told him.

"Great." Todd stuffed the paper into his pocket. "I'll be there around eleven."

Stephanie stared after Todd as he raced down the hall to get to practice.

"Whoa!" Darcy nodded, impressed. "There you go. He finally asked you."

"This is great," Allie cheered. "Every girl in school is totally going to wish she was you on Saturday!"

"You know," Stephanie started. "When you think about it, Todd didn't really ask me to the picnic at all."

Allie frowned. "Stephanie, we were standing right here. Todd wanted your address so he could pick you up on Saturday."

"But he didn't *ask* me if I wanted to go to the picnic with him," Stephanie insisted. "He just assumed I would say yes."

"You *do* want to go with him, though. Right?" Allie pointed out.

"Yeah. But . . ." Stephanie let her words trail off. It was hard for her to put her finger on why she felt so strange about the whole thing.

"Stephanie!" someone called.

She turned and saw Paula rushing toward her, her red ponytail bouncing behind her.

"I didn't mean to eavesdrop, but I just heard what happened," Paula gushed. She gave Stephanie a huge hug. "I can't believe that Todd Barnes asked you to the picnic. That means you're officially dating. You are, like, the luckiest girl in the world!"

Stephanie forced herself to grin. "Thanks."

"I can't wait to tell everyone!" Paula said. She bounded off. "Bye."

"You know, if I'm the luckiest girl in school, why does this whole thing feel wrong?" Stephanie asked her friends.

"Listen, Stephanie. Todd may not be perfect, but nobody is," Darcy stated. "Plus, Todd *is* the most popular boy in school—and he wants to be with *you!*"

Allie glanced at her watch. "Yikes, I have to go! I've got a piano lesson in twenty minutes. Darce, do you need a ride?"

"Sure," Darcy said. She turned toward Stephanie. "We'll talk more tonight if you want. Okay?"

"Sure." Stephanie waved good-bye to her friends. "Later."

Stephanie thought hard as she made her way down the hall. Was she being too sensitive about Todd? Was that why she felt as if he didn't really like her?

"Hi, Stephanie. Mind if I walk home with you?" a boy's voice said. Stephanie turned and saw Ted Bailey standing beside her.

"Sure," Stephanie said. "Any time, Ted."

Stephanie stole a glance at her neighbor from out of the corner of her eye. His new look was startling—but amazing.

With shorter hair and more stylish clothes Ted actually looked—well, cute. With a capital C.

"You look a little worried," Stephanie noticed. "Is something wrong?"

"No, everything's fine," he answered.

Stephanie smiled. She didn't want to burden Ted with her problems, so she quickly got Todd out of her mind. "So," she began, "I know you're a big fan of sci-fi and computers, but what else do you like to do?"

"Actually, I really like to ride horses," Ted admitted.

"Really?" Stephanie gaped at Ted in shock. "I ride, too."

"English or western?" Ted asked.

Stephanie laughed. "You mean, you know the difference?" She was impressed. Most boys knew nothing about horses—except that cowboys rode them in movies.

"Sure," Ted smiled a slow, easygoing grin. "My aunt and uncle have a horse farm in Montana. Whenever we visit them, I have a chance to ride. My mom says I spend more time with the horses than with my family."

Stephanie chuckled. "I ride English mostly," she answered. "But I've ridden western, too."

"I'm strictly western," Ted said. "That English stuff would totally ruin my macho image."

Stephanie laughed out loud as Ted pretended to flex his nonexistent muscles.

Stephanie asked a ton of questions about life on a real horse ranch as the two of them walked home. Ted was so funny and relaxed that a strange thought began to form in Stephanie's head: *Wouldn't it be cool to go to the picnic with Ted?*

But wait a minute. Stephanie already had a

date—with Todd. And hadn't Ted told her that he was thinking of asking someone else, too? She put the thought out of her mind.

"Stephanie." Ted cleared his throat. "I have to ask you, are you going to the picnic on Saturday?"

Stephanie sighed and nodded. "Yeah. Todd's picking me up at eleven. But, Ted, you never told me who you decided to ask. Who's the lucky girl?"

Ted turned pale. "I—uhh—I—" he stammered.

Oh, no, Stephanie thought. *Now I've totally embarrassed him. I bet he never asked the girl he wanted to go with. Or worse—maybe he did ask her and she turned him down.*

Ted quickly pulled himself together. "I'm not even sure if I'm going yet. I've, uh—got a lot of work to catch up on."

"It would be a shame if you missed it," Stephanie told him.

"I'll, uh—have to think about it." Ted shrugged, then turned up the walk to his house. "Well, see you."

"Oh, okay." Stephanie had been having such a great time talking she hadn't noticed that they were already home.

As Stephanie watched Ted vanish through his front door she realized that he was a lot more interesting than she had imagined.

And smarter and cuter and nicer than just about any boy in school, she thought. *If I wasn't already dating Todd, I'd love to spend more time with Ted.*

Troubled, Stephanie continued on to her house. The more she thought about it, the more she realized that—if it wasn't for his wonderful e-mail—she'd stop seeing Todd in a minute.

MICHELLE

Chapter 15

My class is sure going to love me tomorrow, Michelle thought. *Free cookies for everyone— and it isn't even a special occasion!*

She placed a huge plastic container of chocolate chip and walnut cookies next to her book bag at the bottom of the stairs. Making cookies with her dad had taken two hours after dinner. Michelle had a load of fun doing it, but it was also a great way to keep her dad away from the computer.

But now that the cookies were done, Michelle knew she'd have to be on guard again. She needed to be in position to stop her dad in case he tried to get into the study.

The only problem is that I can't think of anything else that will keep him busy, Michelle realized.

She walked into the living room, turned on the TV, and settled back to keep watch. When the phone rang, someone else answered it on the first ring. *Maybe it's Dad's producer from* Wake Up, San Francisco, she hoped. *If Dad has to go to the studio tonight, I'll be home free.*

"It's for you, Michelle." Joey walked in from the kitchen and handed her the cordless phone.

"Thanks." Michelle tried not to show her disappointment. She took the phone from Joey. "What's Dad doing?" she asked, putting her hand over the receiver.

"He's cleaning all traces of cookie dough off the oven," Joey answered.

"Oh." Michelle sighed as Joey went back into the kitchen. She put the phone to her ear. "Hello?"

"Hi, Michelle. It's Ted."

"Ted!" She sat up straight. "What happened with Stephanie?" Michelle knew that Ted had planned on asking Stephanie to the picnic that day.

She didn't want to seem too curious when Stephanie got home that evening, so she hadn't asked her about it. Instead she hung around the bedroom for a while hoping that Stephanie would say something about the class picnic or Ted.

When she didn't, Michelle tried to start a conversation about the picnic. Unfortunately, Stephanie had been too distracted to talk. Her space colony report was due the next day.

"Well, we had a nice talk walking home from school," Ted answered, "but—uhh . . ." he hesitated.

"But what?" Michelle demanded to know. "Did you chicken out?"

"No," Ted said. "I didn't have a chance to. She's going to the class picnic with Todd Barnes."

"She *is?*" Michelle bit her lip. *Maybe I should have told Ted about Todd earlier,* she thought. *If he knew he had competition, he might have asked Stephanie to the picnic sooner.*

"Well, didn't you tell her about the e-mail messages?" Michelle asked. "Does she know that you wrote them?"

"There wasn't much point." Ted sounded even more down than Michelle felt. "If she's dating Todd, she must not care very much about messages."

Michelle didn't know what to say. She had been so sure that Stephanie loved the notes. Stephanie had even *sighed* when she got the one Ted sent Tuesday night.

"Promise me you won't tell her I wrote the e-mails, okay, Michelle?" Ted asked.

"All right." Michelle felt so badly about everything, her voice choked up. "I'm really sorry, Ted. Those e-mails were my idea!"

"It was a good idea, Michelle," Ted said. "I was just crazy to think a great girl like Stephanie would want to go out with me. I mean, who am I compared to the star of the basketball team?"

"You're the nicest boy I know, Ted. And that

means a lot." Michelle paused. "Anyway, I totally let you down, so if you don't want to fix Dad's computer anymore, I understand."

"A deal's a deal, Michelle," Ted answered. "It's not your fault things didn't work out with Stephanie. I'll be over tomorrow to put in the new hard drive and transfer your dad's files—just like I promised."

Now Michelle felt even worse. Ted was the nicest, coolest boy she had ever known. It just wasn't fair for him to be unhappy.

"Are you going to the picnic anyway?" Michelle asked.

"I don't think so," Ted reported. "Look, I've got to go, Michelle. I'll see you right after school tomorrow."

"Okay, thanks. Bye, Ted." Michelle hung up the phone wishing there were something else she could do.

But Stephanie is going to the picnic with Todd now and that's that, she thought sadly.

"Thanks for finishing up, Joey," Danny called as he exited the kitchen. He headed for the front door.

"Where are you going, Dad?" Michelle asked.

"To the car to get my briefcase. I have to balance my checkbook." Danny paused as he opened the door. "That is, unless you have anything else you need my help with?"

"Uh—no." Michelle shook her head. Even if she could think of another problem, her father would definitely get suspicious. She'd have to think of some other reason to keep him away from the computer.

"Good. I'll be right back." Danny headed outside.

Michelle ran to the study door. She didn't have a clue how to keep her dad from going inside. She opened the door and stared into the darkened room. The blank computer monitor seemed to stare back at her.

The solution suddenly hit Michelle. She reached around and turned the lock on the inside of the door. Then she pulled the door shut.

She tried to turn the knob—and the door didn't budge. *Perfect!* she thought. She dashed back into the living room and jumped onto the couch. She picked up a magazine from the side table and pretended to leaf through it.

Danny returned to the house with his briefcase and strode over to the study door.

Michelle held her breath and waited. Several seconds passed before he walked back into the living room.

"What's wrong?" she asked.

"The study door is stuck," Danny answered. "I think the lock is jammed. Do you have any idea how it got that way?"

Michelle shrugged her shoulders.

"You know, if I didn't know better, I'd think that someone was deliberately trying to keep me from doing the household finances," Danny said, frowning.

Someone is, Michelle thought. *Me!*

She felt a little guilty about not confessing to locking the door, but her dad's whole evening would be ruined if he knew the computer didn't work.

Besides, after Ted installs the new hard drive tomorrow, everything will be fine, Michelle told herself. *It has to be.*

"I guess *how* it got locked doesn't matter." Danny shook his head. "We just need to get it open." He picked up the cordless phone from the coffee table. He dialed information and got the number of a locksmith.

Michelle turned the TV on and pretended to watch the screen. But she was really paying attention to her father's conversation—and hoping the locksmith was too busy to come right away.

"No, Mr. Pitman, it's not an emergency." Danny nodded, but he still looked irritated. "Yes, four o'clock tomorrow afternoon will be fine."

Michelle exhaled as her father gave the locksmith their address and hung up. Then he sat on the couch beside her.

"Is there anything good on?" Danny asked when Michelle handed him the TV remote.

"Anything's okay with me," Michelle said.

Danny began to flip through the channels.

Michelle settled back, grinning to herself. Everything was going to be just fine! Todd would be able to fix the computer long before the locksmith opened the door of the study. The computer would be as good as new—and her dad would never have to find out it was broken!

Then a thought occurred to her:

Wait a minute. The study door is locked! How is Ted supposed to get inside to fix the computer if I locked the door!

Okay, don't panic, she coached herself. *Maybe Dad won't be home when the locksmith arrives. In that case, the locksmith can open the door, and Ted can slip into the study to fix the computer.*

But what if her father returned home before the locksmith opened the door—or before Ted could finish the job?

Then, Michelle realized, *I'll be totally busted!*

STEPHANIE

Chapter
16

Stephanie dropped all her books in her room the next day after school. Her term paper about space colonies was done, and she didn't have any other homework. The teachers had obviously decided to give the eighth grade a break since the class picnic was the next day.

Stephanie raced down the stairs. She wanted to make sure that Joey had remembered to get the chips and dip she had volunteered to bring to the picnic.

Stephanie jumped down the last two steps onto the landing. "Free as a bird!" she cheered.

Mr. Pitman, the locksmith, was working on the study door. "You're sure sounding chipper, young lady," he said, glancing up from his work.

"It's Friday!" Stephanie explained.

"Sure is." Mr. Pitman grinned. "And this is my last job of the week. I should be done in a minute."

Today had been an absolutely excellent day for Stephanie. Even lunch with Todd had been kind of fun. He hadn't asked her for a single favor. And he actually seemed excited about going to the picnic!

Maybe the real Todd—the sensitive one she liked in the e-mail messages—was finally starting to come out!

As Stephanie passed by the front door, she saw Ted and Michelle sitting on the front steps.

Stephanie had been so involved with her term paper, she suddenly realized she hadn't let Michelle use the computer all week. Michelle was such a great sister, she hadn't even complained once.

Still grinning, Stephanie bounded out onto the porch to talk to her.

"Hey, Ted. Hey, Michelle," Stephanie called. They turned to look over their shoulders at her.

"Listen, Michelle," Stephanie continued. "You've been so cool about letting me use the computer for my science report, that I wanted to let you know—you can have it all weekend to play your game."

"Great. Thanks." Michelle turned around again to stare at the step beneath her. Her shoulders heaved as she dropped her chin in her hands.

Stephanie paused and frowned. *That's not the enthusiastic response I expected.*

She turned to her next-door neighbor. "What's up with you, Ted?" she asked.

"Not much." Ted gave her a halfhearted wave and sighed.

This looks like trouble, Stephanie thought. *I wonder what's up.*

"Okay, you two," Stephanie said. "Spill the beans. What's wrong?"

Ted glanced at Michelle and shrugged.

Michelle took a deep breath. "I goofed, Stephanie. Really bad."

"Okay." Stephanie nodded. "Well, everyone makes mistakes—and if you tell me about this one, maybe I can help."

Ted nodded. "It can't hurt, Michelle."

"I guess you're right," Michelle agreed. "I know I wasn't supposed to use the computer in the study, Stephanie, but I just wanted to play my game. I didn't mean to break it."

"You *broke* Dad's computer?" Stephanie's eyes widened in disbelief. No wonder her sister was upset!

"Actually, Michelle didn't break it," Ted interjected. "The hard drive was already going bad. Unfortunately, it crashed while Michelle was using the computer."

"I didn't want Dad to know I was using it, when I'm not allowed to." Michelle looked miserable. "So I've been keeping him away from the study the last few days."

"But Dad will be home any minute, Michelle," Stephanie said. "And you can't keep him out of the study forever. Sooner or later, he's going to find out what happened."

"Dad won't find out if Ted gets a chance to

fix the computer," Michelle said. "Ted knows how to put all Dad's files back and everything. He even got Dad a new hard drive with his own money."

Ted raised a small cardboard box. "It came today."

Stephanie was blown away. "Wow, Ted. That's an awful lot of trouble and expense for you to go to for Michelle. I mean, you hardly even know her."

"Actually, we've become pretty good friends." Ted put an arm around Michelle's shoulders and gave her a squeeze. "And friends have to help each other out when they can."

Stephanie studied Ted for a long moment. *I wonder if Todd would be that selfless—even for his best friend!*

"I don't understand," she continued. "If Ted has the hard drive, what's the problem?"

"I'll need a couple hours to install the hard drive and transfer the files from your dad's backup drive." Ted leaned forward and rested his elbows on his knees. "But we had to wait for the locksmith to unlock the door, so I probably won't have enough time before your dad gets home."

"Actually, you don't have any time," Stephanie said as she saw her dad's car turn the corner on to their street.

"Oh, no!" Michelle saw the car, too, and jumped up. "Dad's already here!"

"Of all the rotten luck." Ted shook his head.

Stephanie's brain clicked into high gear. Even though Michelle shouldn't have been using their father's computer, she hadn't deliberately broken it. As Ted said, the hard drive was going to crash anyway. *And since Ted and Michelle are going to fix it, why does Dad have to know?*

"I've got an idea," Stephanie said.

"You do?" Michelle looked up with shining eyes.

Ted raised a curious eyebrow.

"Keep your fingers crossed." Stephanie dashed up to her dad's car when he parked. "Hi, Dad!"

"Hi, Stephanie." Danny waved at Ted and Michelle through the open car window.

"I hate to ask you this, Dad, but I need a huge favor," Stephanie blurted out. "I'm going to the class picnic with the coolest guy in school tomorrow and I don't have anything to wear!"

Danny blinked. "Really? The last time I checked, you didn't have room in your closet to hang one more outfit." His eyes sparkled at his own joke.

"This is serious, Dad," Stephanie insisted.

Her father took a deep breath and frowned. "How important is it to have something new to wear?"

Trick question, Stephanie thought, but she knew the answer. "I'll do all the dishes for two weeks and any extra chores you want."

"It's that important, huh?" Danny smiled.

Stephanie nodded.

"Get in," he told her.

"Thanks, Dad!" Stephanie glanced back at Ted and Michelle as she ran to the passenger side of the car. As she opened the door, she saw Michelle mouth the words "thank you." Ted gave her a thumbs-up.

Now that's a cool guy! Stephanie thought. She slid into the front seat and settled back to think as her father pulled away from the house.

She had liked Ted from the moment she had met him, but she hadn't really thought about him as a potential date. *What a mistake that was!* she admitted to herself. Ted was sweet and sensitive, too, but unlike Todd, he didn't think he had to hide it from everyone.

Stephanie stared out the window. If she wasn't already going to the picnic with Todd, Ted would have been the perfect date.

MICHELLE

Chapter
17

Michelle finished drying the Saturday morning breakfast dishes and stood back to survey her work.

"Great job, Michelle," Uncle Jesse said. "But I thought Stephanie was supposed to do the dishes."

"Well, I kind of owe her a big favor," Michelle explained. "And I wanted to do the dishes this morning so Stephanie could get ready for the class picnic."

Michelle was so grateful that Stephanie had kept their dad busy at the mall the day before.

While they were gone, Ted installed the new hard drive in her dad's computer. Thanks to Stephanie, she wasn't in trouble anymore. She would have done eight million dishes to say thank you for that.

Michelle paused at the study door and looked inside. Danny was sitting at his desk using the computer to get all his accounts up to date. *And the computer is working perfectly!* Michelle realized. *Ted is a genius.*

Thinking about Ted made Michelle sad. He had helped her just the way he said he would. It was too bad Michelle couldn't keep her side of the bargain.

The doorbell rang. Stephanie was still upstairs, her father was busy, and nobody else was around. "I'll get it!" Michelle bellowed to the rest of the house.

She ran to the door and opened it. She wasn't surprised to see the same tall, blond boy that had been with Stephanie at the mall standing on the other side. He was wearing shorts with a lot of pockets and a T-shirt with a basketball team logo.

Wow. He really is cute, Michelle thought, staring at him. Then she remembered not to be impolite. "Hi." She smiled. "Are you Todd?"

"Yeah." Todd scowled and looked over Michelle's head into the house. "Where's Stephanie?"

He just got here. Why does he look so annoyed? Michelle wondered.

"I thought she'd be waiting for me outside," Todd snapped. "I told her I'd be here at eleven."

Outside? Michelle thought. Every other boy Stephanie went out with came to the door to pick her up!

"Hi, Todd!" Stephanie called as she ran down the stairs carrying a large straw beach bag. She stopped to pick up the grocery bags with the chips and dip Joey had left on the coffee table for her.

Michelle thought her sister looked great. Stephanie was wearing her new, dark blue shorts, which also had a lot of pockets, and a cream-colored pullover sweater with a

V-neck. Her slouch socks matched the top, and her sneakers matched her shorts.

"Hurry up, my big brother's waiting in the car," Todd said. He turned and ran down the porch steps.

Michelle watched as a frown formed on Stephanie's face. She sighed, then headed for the door. "See you later," she called.

"Okay." Michelle watched as Todd hopped into the front seat of the waiting car and slammed the door closed. Stephanie had her arms full and had to drop the beach bag to open the back door. She even had to push Todd's stuff over before she could get inside.

Michelle waved as the car pulled away, but she was really bothered by Todd's behavior. He hadn't said hello or told Stephanie that she looked nice.

And he should have helped Stephanie with all her stuff, Michelle decided. *How could Stephanie like someone who's so rude?* She thought about it on the way upstairs to her bedroom.

She had the computer all to herself to play 'Marla's Magical Mystery,' but that didn't seem very important right now. She knew Stephanie better than anyone, except maybe D.J. and their father. Why was she acting so strangely?

Todd is good-looking, but he's a jerk! Michelle thought.

Totally bewildered, Michelle sat down at the computer. *Since I can't do anything about Stephanie's love life, I might as well play my game while I can.*

Michelle hadn't played 'Marla's Magical Mystery' in days and couldn't find its CD case. She lifted Stephanie's books to check underneath them.

A notebook slid off the top of the pile and landed on the floor. Some papers slipped out of the binder.

Whoops! Michelle knelt down to put everything back where it was—and noticed the e-mail messages from Ted that Stephanie had printed out. There was writing on one of the pages.

Curious, she picked it up. It was the very first note that Ted had sent.

Michelle read the scribbled writing and gasped. "Oh, no!"

Stephanie had written "Todd Barnes" next to the initials *TB*. She had also written "basketball team number" beside *03*.

Michelle couldn't believe it. Stephanie didn't know TB03 stood for Ted Bailey the Third. She thought Todd Barnes had sent Ted's messages!

I bet that's *why Stephanie likes Todd. She thinks that Todd is Ted!* Michelle laughed and ran for the phone. *This is excellent! Maybe I can pay Ted back after all!*

Chapter 18

Stephanie hardly said anything on the drive to the park. Todd's older brother seemed nice, but he and Todd spent most of the ride talking about sports.

Todd's brother tried to include her in the conversation, but she was too deep in thought to be interested. She didn't know why Todd was so irritated, but it was no excuse for being rude to her.

To put it mildly, their date had not gotten off to a very good start.

In a few minutes the car pulled up to the

local park where John Muir held its annual class picnic.

"Oh, there's Allie and Darcy!" Stephanie exclaimed. She waved when her friends saw her. George and Doug were there, too, and all four of them were helping a teacher arrange things on the food tables.

Todd grunted and pointed toward two tables near the park basketball court. "The guys are over there."

"Right." Stephanie rolled her eyes. The team was already warming up on the court while their dates, including Paula and Melinda, sat at the tables and watched.

Stephanie glanced around. A lot of kids were already swimming in the lake or paddling canoes under teacher supervision. A volleyball net had been set up and a game was in progress. The teams were mixed—boys and girls, Stephanie noticed. A few other kids were dancing to a CD playing on a boom box.

Would she and Todd be doing any of that stuff? she wondered.

Not unless Todd snapped out of his bad

mood and changed into 'e-mail guy' soon, she realized. Deep down, Stephanie was still hoping that would happen. Todd's notes had been too sincere to be some horrible joke.

"Hey, Todd!" John yelled and waved.

Todd ran toward his friend, leaving Stephanie to lug her grocery bags and beach bag by herself. *At least, he didn't ask me to carry his bag, too*, she thought.

"Hi, Stephanie." Paula smiled when Stephanie got to the table. "How are you doing?"

"Okay, I guess," she answered.

"What did you bring?" Melinda craned her neck to peek inside the grocery bag. "Chips and dip! Cool. I'm starved."

"Yeah. Watching other people play basketball really works up an appetite." Stephanie was joking, but Melinda didn't catch on.

"I'll say." She ripped open a bag of chips and dug in. "Have a seat."

"In a minute." Stephanie stashed her beach bag under the table.

"What's in there?" Melinda asked, glancing at Stephanie's bag.

"Bathing suit, beach towel, sunscreen," Stephanie said. "You're all going swimming later, aren't you?"

"With these guys?" Paula laughed. "No way!"

"They'll play basketball until they drop," Melinda said. "With time out to eat, of course."

Stephanie paused to stare at Todd. He looked totally cool as he dribbled the basketball and made a fantastic shot from mid-court. The ball fell neatly through the hoop.

"Way to shoot, Todd!" Melinda cheered. Then she and Paula jumped up. They started one of their cheerleading routines.

Todd just kept playing.

What good is having a date who doesn't pay any attention to me? Stephanie asked herself.

At that moment a major thought occurred to her. It didn't matter if everyone else thought she was lucky to be on a date with Todd—or that he wrote sweet e-mails. If she was miserable, what was the point?

"Come on, Stephanie!" Melinda waved her

over. "We'll teach you a couple of the squad's routines."

"Sure. When I get back." *If I get back,* Stephanie thought. She started toward the food tables to see her friends.

Todd called after her. "Hey, Stephanie, as long as you're going over there, bring me back a soda, okay?"

Stephanie looked back with a tight smile. That was the last straw. "You're going to get awfully thirsty if you count on me to get your drinks, Todd Barnes," she muttered to herself. She ran over to Allie and Darcy.

"Hi, Stephanie!" Allie set a big bowl of pasta salad on the table. "Is that a new outfit?"

"It looks great." Darcy nodded with approval.

"We're going to play some catch when we're done here," Doug said. "You can join us if you want, Stephanie."

"Thanks. I just might take you up on that." Stephanie smiled, then whispered to Darcy. "Can I talk to you and Allie? Alone?"

Her two friends excused themselves, then

walked with Stephanie to a large bench under a shady tree.

"What's up?" Allie asked. She sat on the bench beside Stephanie.

"Yeah." Darcy sat on the ground in front of them. "Aren't you here with Todd?"

Stephanie cocked her head. "That's just it. I am here with him, but Todd is never really *with* anyone except the guys on the basketball team."

Stephanie took a deep breath, then continued. "I've been hanging out with Todd for a week, but most of the time he doesn't care whether I'm there or not—unless he *needs* something. All he really cares about is basketball and messing around with his friends."

Darcy and Allie both looked toward the basketball court. Todd and the team were playing hard.

Stephanie sighed. "Todd wouldn't even know that I'm gone, except that he asked me to get him a soda."

"Shouldn't he be getting you a soda half the time?" Allie asked. "I mean, you are his date."

"Exactly," Stephanie said. "At first I thought you guys were right—that Todd was just shy and didn't want to act as though he liked me in front of his friends. But now I don't think that's the problem at all."

"So what is the problem?" Darcy asked.

"I don't know." Stephanie shook her head. "But I'm *really* tired of being ignored—or treated like Todd's personal waitress."

"His e-mails were so thoughtful and sweet." Allie looked even more confused. "I don't understand this at all."

"Neither do I," Stephanie said. "It's like dealing with two different people."

"Maybe you should ask Todd about it," Darcy suggested.

Stephanie exhaled and nodded. She should have asked Todd about the e-mails a long time ago. *Well,* she thought, *better late than never.*

She marched back to the basketball court—right into the middle of the game.

"What are you doing, Stephanie?" Todd asked, annoyed. "You're in the way."

"We have to talk." Stephanie looked him in the eye.

Todd hesitated, then cast a glance at the other players. They were all watching with intense interest.

Stephanie didn't care who heard what she had to say, but Todd apparently didn't want to discuss things in front of an audience.

"All right." Sighing, Todd tossed the ball to Ty and followed Stephanie to a vacant table.

Stephanie sat next to Todd on the nearest bench. "Clear something up for me," she demanded. "Tell me how you can be so nice and caring in your e-mails and such a loser in person."

Todd just stared at her. He looked almost as puzzled as Allie had a few minutes ago. "E-mails?" he asked.

Stephanie blinked. "You know, the ones you sent to Stepper, my e-mail address."

Todd shrugged. "I never sent you any e-mails. I didn't even know your address until you just told me."

"Hold on. You're not TB03?"

Todd shook his head. "No. Now, can I get back to playing ball?"

Stephanie's mind reeled. *No wonder Todd seems like a different person in his e-mail. He is a different person in his e-mail! And the e-mail guy is the one I really like. So what am I doing here with Todd?*

"Yo, Stephanie? Can I get back to my game now?" Todd interrupted her thoughts. "I'm a little tired of sitting here arguing with my date."

"Consider yourself off the hook," Stephanie told him coolly. "Because as of this moment, I'm your ex-date."

"What?" Todd looked totally shocked. "Wait a minute. Are you dumping me?"

"You've got it." Stephanie stood up and walked away. The other girls at the basketball team tables stared at her as she grabbed her beach bag and began to leave the table.

Paula caught up to Stephanie before she had gone too far. "What happened, Stephanie? Did you and Todd have a fight?"

"Actually, I just broke up with him." Stephanie shrugged.

"You did?" Paula's mouth fell open.

Stephanie nodded. She didn't really want to talk about it.

"Gee, I'm sorry," Paula told her.

"Don't be," Stephanie stated. "It's for the best." Then she remembered something. "Oh, and I wanted to let you know, I won't be trying out for the cheerleading squad on Wednesday. I'm just too busy to take on any new extracurricular activities."

"I'm sorry to hear that, too." Paula really did look disappointed. "You would have been perfect."

Stephanie felt a little better knowing that Paula, Melinda, and the other girls had wanted her on the squad for herself—even if the idea only came to them after they thought Todd was interested in her.

Stephanie wandered back toward the food tables, searching for Darcy and Allie. It would be good to talk to her friends about the whole crazy incident. She felt so foolish, hanging out with Todd even though he acted like a jerk.

Stephanie caught sight of her friends. They

were having a great time playing catch with George and Doug.

I don't want to ruin their fun because I'm feeling awful, she thought. At that moment she wished she could find Ted. He was easy to talk to and so funny, he'd probably have her laughing at herself in no time. *And he won't make me feel like a complete idiot, either.* She scanned the whole picnic area, but she didn't see Ted anywhere.

Dragging her beach bag, Stephanie returned to the bench under the shade tree and sat down. She didn't think anything could possibly lift her spirits.

Then it occurred to her that one very important question hadn't been answered.

If Todd Barnes didn't send her those wonderful e-mails, who did?

MICHELLE

Chapter
19

Michelle thanked Joey for driving her and
Ted to the park. Then she jumped out of the
car. "Come on, Ted!"

"Okay, I'm coming!" Ted slid out of the
backseat.

"Should I wait for you?" Joey asked after
Ted closed the back door.

"Yes, please," Michelle told Joey. "I'll be
leaving soon. Ted won't."

"Okay." Joey turned his radio up a few
notches and began bopping to the music. "I'll
be right here."

"Let's go," Michelle said and took Ted's hand. "Stephanie said the class picnic was being set up near the lake."

They didn't have to go far. Michelle soon spotted Stephanie sitting under a tree—alone.

"Check it out, Ted." Michelle pointed toward her sister. "Stephanie's by herself—and Todd's nowhere in sight."

Ted took a deep breath and followed Michelle up the rise toward the tree. They quickened their pace, then stopped short.

Todd came bounding up to Stephanie from the other direction.

"What do you want, Todd?" Michelle heard Stephanie say.

Normally, Michelle knew she shouldn't eavesdrop on a private conversation, but this was important!

"Maybe we'd better go," Ted whispered.

Michelle grabbed his sleeve as he started to turn. "No! Just wait," she whispered back.

"What do I want?" Todd sounded really mad. "I just wanted to let you know that I told everyone *I* broke up with you. Nobody will ever believe you dumped me."

Stephanie just shrugged. "As long as we're over, I don't care what anyone thinks."

You tell him, Stephanie! Michelle couldn't help smiling.

"Fine! Have fun by yourself." Todd turned and stalked off.

Michelle glanced at Ted. He was staring at Stephanie in disbelief. "Your turn," she told him.

Ted coughed. "Okay. I guess it can't hurt to try."

Stephanie caught sight of Ted and Michelle just before they reached her spot on the bench. "Hey, Ted! I wondered where you were," she called.

"You did?" Ted swallowed hard. "I mean, I had a few things to do before I came."

"Are you . . . with anybody?" Stephanie asked.

"Just Michelle," Ted told her.

Stephanie glanced down. "What are you doing here?"

"Just hanging out for a minute." Michelle gave Stephanie her most innocent-looking smile.

"Joey drove us over," Ted explained.

"Oh." Stephanie cocked her head to study Ted. For a while no one said anything.

When the silence started to last too long, Michelle blurted out, "Ted's got something to tell you, Stephanie."

"Oh?" Stephanie gave Ted a curious glance. "What?"

"Well, I—uh—thought you should know that . . ." Ted cleared his throat.

Michelle couldn't stand it. "Ted is TB03, Stephanie! He's the one who wrote the e-mails you've been getting."

"He *is*?" Stephanie's eyes lit up.

"Ted Bailey the Third," Ted shrugged. "That's me."

"Wow! I can't believe it!" Stephanie looked at Michelle and frowned. "Wait a minute—how do you know about those e-mails, Michelle?"

"They were my idea." Michelle slapped her hand over her mouth. "Oops."

"What?" Stephanie looked stunned.

"Maybe I'd better explain." Ted adjusted his glasses and sat down. "The truth is that I really like you, Stephanie, but I didn't have the nerve to tell you. Michelle suggested that I e-mail you. She was just trying to help."

"Right." Michelle nodded.

"I see." Stephanie paused. "Well, I think I should tell you something, too, Ted."

"What?" Ted tensed.

"The only reason I liked Todd in the first place was because I thought he wrote those wonderful e-mails," she admitted.

I knew it! Michelle thought.

"Allie, Darcy, and I used the school directory to try to figure out who TB03 was," Stephanie explained. "We thought it was Todd because of his initials and his basketball team number. We didn't even think about Ted Bailey the *Third*, because he isn't in the directory!"

She turned toward Ted. "You weren't registered at John Muir when the school year started, so you weren't included in the student directory."

Ted laughed. "That is funny!"

Michelle caught Ted's eye and motioned for him to bring up the *big* question.

"So will you be my date for the rest of the picnic, Stephanie?" he asked smoothly.

"Yes. I thought you'd never ask," Stephanie cheered.

She squeezed Ted's hand, then turned back to Michelle. "I should be furious with you for interfering in my love life, little sister."

"Are you?" Michelle asked timidly.

"No." Stephanie reached out and pulled Michelle onto the bench. "I should be, but if it wasn't for you I wouldn't have a date with the most terrific guy in the eighth grade."

Ted grinned.

"Cool." Michelle's heart swelled. Everything worked out better than she had hoped. Stephanie and Ted were together—and she wasn't in trouble for breaking her father's computer.

"Thanks for keeping Dad busy yesterday so Ted could fix the computer, Stephanie," Michelle said.

"No problem," Stephanie said. "But don't touch Dad's computer again, okay? Or you'll be grounded for years."

"Promise." Michelle crossed her heart.

Stephanie gave Michelle a big hug. "What would I ever do without you?"

"Don't worry about that," Michelle said. "We're stuck with each other—we're sisters!"

FULL HOUSE™
Michelle

A MINSTREL® BOOK
Published by Pocket Books

1033-34

Don't miss out on any of
Stephanie and Michelle's
exciting adventures!

FULL HOUSE™
Sisters

When sisters get together...
expect the unexpected!

A MINSTREL® BOOK
Published by Pocket Books

2012-05